The Viking's Son

By

Marti Talbott

Cover art: Yocla Designs

All of Marti Talbott's Books are suitable for ages 14 and above.

www.martitalbott.com

From the back cover:

Donaldina's mother died when she was four, or so her father said. She suspected something was amiss but never knew what, and now that she was old enough, her father was determined to marry her off. Always before, she managed to waylay his wedding attempts, and when Laird Wallace MacGreagor came to buy spices from her clan, she fully intended to avoid it this time too.

CHAPTER 1

Donald Bisset was a ruthless laird who ruled over vast lands and a clan of nearly one thousand in the south of Scotland. Few were left idle, for the clan either grew or bartered with the English, spices they could sell at higher prices to the Scottish clans in the north. It was a lucrative business indeed, and Laird Bisset had all a man could possibly want. His castle offered a magnificent view of his land, he had warehouses filled with goods he accepted as barter, and the village and castle were surrounded by a tall, spiked fence with a watchtower on each of four corners. The more valuable items were kept in the Great Hall of his castle for his customers to admire. He was young, called handsome by women who favored his tan skin and light hair, owned the best weapons, and wore ruby and diamond rings on his fingers.

His first wife was not a woman of his choosing, but rather a way of making peace with a neighboring clan. He treated her well enough and was grateful for the three strong sons she gave him, yet he was not altogether sorry when she died trying to deliver his fourth child.

It was his second wife with whom he fell completely and hopelessly in love. The tall, pretty woman with hair the same color of his, had a way of soothing his ire, and loved him with a passion he never knew existed. Therefore, he was overjoyed when he heard she had given him twin daughters. As soon as the midwife let him into the bedchamber on the second floor of his castle, he went to the first wooden box and looked adoringly at the fair-haired baby. But when he viewed the second child, a vile rage surged up in him, for the hair of the second child was dark.

He spun around and shouted, "You have deceived me!"

In her bed, his confused wife trembled as he slowly and deliberately came toward her. "Husband, what do you accuse me of?"

"You know very well what you have done. The first is mine, but the second child cannae be!" He pointed at the second box and then yelled, "I banish you and take that wee bairn with you. Be gone within the hour or suffer the full measure of my wrath!"

"But where can I go?" she cried. Her question went unanswered. Instead he abruptly walked out and slammed the door so hard one of the hinges broke.

It was far too soon, having just given birth, but she did as he commanded. In the castle courtyard, and with her second baby in her arms, the despondent woman sat upon her horse and looked up at the window where her husband stood watching. She hoped beyond hope that he would change his mind.

The wooden fence kept spice thieves and wild animals alike from entering, but just now the double gates were wide open. Word of her crime spread quickly, and hundreds had already gathered to watch their mistress take her leave. Some judged her guilty and frowned, while others knew her to be innocent and clearly felt the loss of a woman they had come to love and admire. In silence, they saw her turn her horse, and then gazed after her as she begrudgingly passed through. Too soon, the Bisset warriors sedately closed the gates behind her.

With tears running down her cheeks, the woman halted, turned her horse around a second time, and looked up once more at the castle. Inside was her first born, whom she might never see again, and whom she already missed most desperately. At length, there was nothing to be done, so she turned her horse back around and rode south.

After she was gone, Laird Bisset named his remaining daughter Donaldina after himself, and passed an edict – the clan was never to speak of it, Donaldina was to be told her mother died, and she was never to know about her twin. That night, he drank heavily and once his men had hauled him up to his empty bed, the master of all that lay before him cried out, "What have I done?"

Each day, he came to regret his decision more and more, for he truly loved his wife and would have forgiven her anything…in time. Therefore, when he discovered she had left a Roman coin in the baby's wooden box, he saw it as a sign that someday she might come back. He took the coin to the blacksmith, had a hole put in the top of it, and then threaded a thin leather string through the hole. An odd thing happened when he loosely tied it to the newborn's ankle –

Donaldina smiled. In response, he picked the baby up, kissed the softness of her cheek, and vowed he would let no harm come to her.

Thus began a bond between father and daughter like no other.

In the months that followed, his wife did not return, so Laird Bisset secretly sent men both north and south to see if they could find her. It was to no avail. A year passed and then another before he knew all hope was lost, set his wife aside, and remarried.

Yet he was a troubled man, for someday Donaldina would be old enough to ask questions and his word might not be good enough. Therefore, to further cover the error of his ways, he erected a stone for his missing wife in the graveyard. He reasoned that as long as everyone obeyed his edict, she would never find out and come to despise him for it.

Unfortunately, even his edict could not prevent gossip and gossip was never limited to adults alone. Sooner than he imagined, the next generation learned the truth.

*

It was foretold that Mairi Bisset would be the most beautiful woman any man had ever seen. It was foretold, that is, before she was born. Even as a child, she was quite lovely and as she grew, the prophecy was clearly coming true. However, Mairi took the many compliments to heart and soon became so prideful she was rejected by all the other children.

Donaldina had the same problem, albeit for a different reason. The younger generation sometimes overheard what they ought not to. Because of it, parents kept their children well away for fear one of them would tell. Even her older brothers, and later her younger siblings shunned her. It was, she decided, because her father loved her more than the others. Yet, guessing why did nothing to remedy her heartfelt loneliness. Therefore when Mairi befriended her, ten-year-old Donaldina was elated.

The Bisset clan was just as diverse as any other, with members who suffered shyness, talked too much, or said things that endeared them to no one. Mairi became one of those, for what she said was usually somewhat exaggerated, if not an outright lie. Donaldina didn't seem to mind, in fact, she found Mairi's propensity to manipulate fascinating. Besides, Mairi's antics did not seriously harm anyone. Yet, the day came when Mairi heard the gossip and told Donaldina that her mother was not truly dead. The revelation sent Donaldina screaming into the castle to confront her father.

"She is lying," Laird Bisset claimed. "Does she not always lie?"

"Aye, Father," she answered through quivering lips with tears running down her cheeks.

"Then you must not believe her. Have I not shown you where your mother is buried?"

Donaldina hung her head. "Aye, Father."

"I tell you true, your mother is not alive." He believed it himself and had for years. After all, his wife did not come back, she was nowhere to be found, and therefore she had to be dead. Donaldina was convinced finally, so he kissed the softness of her cheek as he did every day in memory of his love for her mother, and sent her upstairs.

Laird Bisset held his smile until his daughter disappeared around a corner and then narrowed his eyes. In a rage, he left his castle, stomped down one path and then another, until he sought out the child called Mairi. "Where is she?" he demanded as he burst through a cottage door.

Mairi's mother trembled and tried to hide her daughter behind her, but it was no use. Laird Bisset grabbed the girl's arm, pulled her around, and then struck her with the back of his hand. "You are never to go near my daughter again, do you hear?"

With her hand Mairi covered the deep cut his ring left in her cheek and began to cry. "Aye." Blood trickled over her fingers and then ran down her neck.

The harm he caused to the child shocked even him for a moment, but he soon considered it a good thing. "Let her face remind the lot of you not to do what she has done." With that, he stormed back out of the cottage and went home.

In a few weeks, the wound healed, but Mairi was lovely no more.

As she was commanded, she stayed away from Donaldina and as the years passed, she slowly withdrew from the rest of society. Her pride became bitterness and her bitterness became thoughts of revenge. All she had to do was await the perfect opportunity.

*

Laird Bisset's third wife pleased him a little, but he still longed
for Donaldina's mother. Because of it, he drank more and became
more belligerent and demanding. As the years passed, the lonely
Donaldina entertained herself by watching her father barter with the
northern clans. Once, he even asked her opinion, to which she said,
"Father, we have more horses than is reasonable to feed, but I do fancy
the brown filly."

"If that be the case, it shall be yours."

For three bags of salt, Donaldina had a horse of her own. She
named the filly, Arwen, and Arwen became her best and only friend.
While the horse grew into a fine mare, Donaldina grew into a shrewd,
albeit a compassionate young woman, with hair and eyes the color of
her father's.

When his third wife passed, Laird Bisset put his hope of
happiness in a fourth wife. Not but two weeks after that joyful
wedding, his fourth wife died of the fever. He was resigned, for he was
never again to be as happy as he had been with his second wife. Yet,
loneliness vexed him almost as much as it tormented his daughter.

When he married for the fifth time, there arose a spirit of jealousy
in, Tearlag, his new wife that threatened to make the entire clan
miserable. She openly hated the sight of Donaldina, degraded her at
every opportunity, and constantly interfered in their close relationship.

"Marry her off," Tearlag stubbornly demanded, "and see that she goes far, far away."

Laird Bisset repeatedly refused until he grew tired of the constant tussle, and had not the fortitude for their daily arguments. "You break my heart, lass," he told his wife as he bowed his head.

"Better your heart than her head."

He feared it might come to that, for his daughter was just as fixed in her opinions as his wife, and Donaldina delighted in fighting back. For all their sakes, and to have peace again in his castle, he saw no choice but to do what his wife insisted.

*

It took four women and her stepmother to get Donaldina into the abominable, purple English gown she had never seen before. Once that was accomplished, they held her down, braided her long hair, and piled it on the top of her head. When they tried to add flowers with long stems to hold the braid in place, she finally broke free.

"'Tis to make you look more pleasing," her stepmother barked.

Donaldina rolled her eyes. Why on earth would she want to look pleasing? It was the fourth time in as many weeks that her father had her dressed in the gown, and demanded she take a husband. Each time, her stepmother tried to make her look more pleasing, and she could think of nothing more revolting then…or now. It was all for naught anyway, for she had no intention of marrying this time either.

No matter how earnestly she tried to talk her father out of it, Donaldina Bisset found herself standing next to a man much taller than any man had a right to be, and stomped her foot on the wooden floor of her father's Keep. "Nay, I will not have him." The man who agreed to marry her, allowed himself a loud sigh of relief, which caused her to turn and stare at him. He, on the other hand, ignored her.

Directly behind her, with a firm grasp on both of her shoulders lest she bolt and run as she was prone to do, her father was just as determined and said to the priest, "Ask again, Father." This husband, he believed, was the perfect one for her, and Laird Bisset meant to see her married off if it took all day.

The hour was so early, even the cows had not yet bawled to be milked. The strangers wanted to get an early start, so there she was, standing in front of a priest before the crack of dawn. Candles lit the dark Great Hall, casting eerie dancing shadows on the walls – no doubt a forecast of the future she was to have, if she allowed the marriage to take place. The room was filled with members of her beloved clan, who came for no other reason than to see how Donaldina would get out of it this time. Happily, they placed their wagers the night before and few bet that she would give herself in marriage to this man either. Her father always bet that she would – and always lost.

The priest cleared his throat, "Wilt thou have this…"

When the priest asked yet again, she shook her head. The next time he asked, she exaggeratedly sighed and forced tears to come to her eyes. She tried to turn toward her father so he would see them and take pity on her, but this time he would not allow her to turn. Peeved, she instead glared at the man beside her. "He dinna want me and I dinna want him. Nay, I will not marry him this day or any other!"

Donaldina could not believe it. Wallace MacGreagor, or so he called himself, smugly folded his arms and nodded in agreement... as if he had not already given his part of the vow. How dare he so openly reject her in front of her clan? No other man ever had.

Her father's voice loudly boomed across the room, "Ask again, Father!"

The nervous priest visibly jumped, "Please, wilt thou take this lad to be thy husband?"

Dawn was beginning to cast its first light, lessening the shadows on the wall, but it did nothing to improve the looks of the man standing next to her. After a long moment, she tore her eyes away from the rude, insolent man, softened her voice, and tried her best to convince the priest instead. "I most certainly will not and let that be an end to it!" To her amazement, when she looked, the bridegroom's pompous smile was so wide, she could see his teeth. It so enraged her, that upon the very next time the priest asked if she would have him, she put her hands on her hips, looked her intended right in the eye, and said, "Aye."

Just as she hoped, it wiped that irritating, sanctimonious smile right off his face.

It was only after the relieved priest made the sign of the cross that she fully realized what she had done. "I DINNA MEAN IT!" she shouted.

It was too late, for at the slight nod of her husband's head, one of MacGreagor's guards lifted her up, carried her out the door, and set her on her waiting horse. As soon as her husband was mounted on his horse, the guard gave her reins to him, and no matter how loud her protests, not one in her clan came to her rescue. In fact, they were all laughing and shouting as if it were some sort of joyous occasion. The cows began to bawl, the dogs barked, and Donaldina had never been so infuriated.

While the Bisset men finished loading sacks filled with leather spice jars and food for their journey on the backs of the MacGreagor horses, she slid down and ran. Far too easily, the same annoying guard captured her and put her back on her horse. By then, and thanks to the stepmother she hated, all that she owned had been put in a sack and handed to another of her husband's guards.

The second time she attempted to escape, her father grabbed her. He kissed her cheek and whispered in her ear. "Promise you shall try to be happy."

She was too mad to promise him anything, as he none too carefully helped the guard set her once more atop her horse. If that were not bad enough, her father gave her sword and dagger to her husband. She was appalled. Laird Bisset was not even going to let her fight her way out of this mess.

"Put a hand to her backside if needs be," her father told her husband.

The MacGreagor, Donaldina noticed, appeared to take far too much pleasure in that idea, for there was a definite gleam in his eye. She searched for yet another means of escape, but before she could discover one, the MacGreagors began to move. Her husband's guards surrounded her as they passed through the gates, and all she could do was hold on to the mane of her horse to keep from falling off.

Twice, she looked back at her father's face. The first time he was smiling, but the second time, he appeared sorry to see her go. She found no solace in his final expression, for he should have considered that long before he forced her to marry. After they rounded the small pond, she again looked back just long enough to watch the fenced village she loved disappear behind the trees. It was the only home she had ever known and she truly had been happy there, save for her stepmother's meddling. She loved the animals, the music of the flute player, her father's smile, and most of all watching the wild flowers bloom.

Now, she would never see happiness again.

CHAPTER 2

Mairi witnessed Donaldina's marriage from the back of the Keep and like everyone else she was shocked that the marriage actually took place. She watched the MacGreagor guard carry Donaldina out and set her on her horse. She prayed the girl would not make good her escape, and was glad when she didn't. The day of the Laird Bisset's reckoning had finally come.

All she had to do was catch up and tell Donaldina the truth.

She had no doubt Donaldina would return to the village to confront her father, and Mairi fully intended to be there when she did. After that, the young woman with the horrible scar on her face intended to ask if she could join Clan MacGreagor, where she might find a husband of her own. Excited, she rushed to her cottage, gathered her belongings, and then went to the meadow to catch her horse.

*

In an upstairs window of the castle, Tearlag, the fifth wife of Laird Bisset stood beside her brother, Nathair, watching Mairi chase after her horse. Their father was a common field worker, and from a very young age, Tearlag often gazed at the outside of the castle and imagined what it would be like to be mistress of it all. Her design on Laird Bisset was deliberate, and by the time she was old enough to marry, the timing was perfect – Laird Bisset just happened to be without a wife.

Now, she had it all – a husband she could tolerate when necessary, servants to see to all her needs and wants, and a castle to live in. Yet, she found wealth addictive and desired still more in the way of fine garments, gold, silver, and jewels. She could have them too, if she could get rid of her husband's useless daughter, who was forever advising her father not to raise the spice prices. Donaldina was too softhearted and feared the northern clans would have to go without. Tearlag could not have cared less about the northern clans, or any other save her own.

Donaldina was finally gone, but now Mairi threatened to ruin all of Tearlag's plans. "She means to tell Donaldina the truth."

"Aye," Nathair muttered, "and Donaldina will convince her husband to bring her back."

"We cannae let that happen. My husband will think himself pitiful and so beholden for what he did; he would likely bestow half his land on her husband."

Nathair frowned, "If Donaldina comes back, we must kill her."

Tearlag was aghast and turned to face him. "For which he will blame me. I have made no secret of my hatred of his child, and I dinna wish to lose my head over the matter. You must stop Mairi."

He thoughtfully stroked his short beard. "And what are you willing to bestow on me in return?"

"Second in command, if I can persuade him."

"Above his sons?"

She snickered. "His lazy sons, you mean?"

Nathair chuckled, nodded, and then hurried out the door. He had things of his own to gather and a horse to catch.

*

Still holding fast to her horse's mane, it appeared Wallace MacGreagor had no intention of letting her have her reins anytime soon, and each moment took her farther from her home. Two of the guards rode in front of the newly married couple and four rode behind, but if she had control of her horse, she doubted any of them could catch her...if she had control of her horse.

The road north from the Bisset village was well traveled and wide enough for carts and narrow wagons. Yet, the scattered clumps of forest and the pastel blue, pink, and green rolling hills in the intermittent moors offered little protection. The MacGreagors knew all too well that there was much to fear in the unfamiliar southern lands of Scotland. More often than not, thieves waited for men to leave the Bisset village, bided their time, and then attacked in an effort to steal the spices. Soon, but not soon enough to please Wallace, they would enter the thick forest where they would be safer.

Laird Wallace MacGreagor was the eldest son of Stefan, the first MacGreagor laird. Dressed similarly to all Scots, he wore off-white leggings with leather laced around his calves, a gray tunic that hung down to his knees, a wide belt, and a warm bearskin cloak he could easily shed when the sun warmed the earth. As well, he wore a large gold medallion around his neck, and leather bands on each forearm to strengthen his wrists in times of battle. He carried a bow over his shoulder, an arrow sheath on his back, and strings tied around his waist kept his dagger and sword at the ready. Now, of course, he had her weapons tied around his waist too, and in his free hand, he held the reins of her horse.

Donaldina spoke not a word for quite a while as they continued to cross the hills and dales, which even she found rather odd for one who could not stop speaking during the ceremony. Her father once said a silent woman was normally a plotting one and that was certainly true in this case. When she wasn't planning her escape, she thought to kill the MacGreagors off one by one.

Just then, her husband glanced back at her, no doubt to see the expected tears in her eyes. That was one sight she would never let him see, even though she was mad enough to cry. In return she left no question in his mind as to her disposition. If he thought her dangerous, so much the better, for all women were dangerous when they felt trapped. A marriage without love was a trap indeed.

"Are you not cold?" he asked

At first she turned her face away and ignored him. Of course she was. Her stepmother neglected to give her a warm cape to wear, no doubt on purpose. On second thought, she sarcastically muttered, "How kind of you to ask." He brazenly turned his back to her.

"I wish to go home," said she, to which he made no reply. "I demand you take me back!" Again, he said nothing. "Give me my weapons and my horse, and I shall go back on my own. I am quite capable of protecting myself." She watched what she could see of the side of his face, and noticed he held his jaw rigid. It was a good sign she might be winning. "If you dinna let me go, I shall see that you live a life of misery."

Apparently, he was not impressed. Each minute took her further and further from her home and she had to come up with something that would work. "I warn you, I dinna cook, and I know not how to wash the clothes. I am spoiled you see, having servants all my years. And another thing, although I hated my stepmother, I learned her devices well. Therefore, I know just how to make myself unbearable. I am…" Donaldina went on and on, getting not one response, and just when she was about to run out of things to threaten, he finally turned to look at her.

"I care not what you do."

Donaldina lifted her eyes to the heavens and rapidly blinked her annoyance. The ridiculous purple gown was so full in the skirt that it nearly spread out over the entire top of her horse. It was so heavy that she pitied her horse almost as much as she pitied herself. The garb was to keep her safe on the journey, her father said that morning, for few were the Scots who wanted an English woman. That he cared for her safety endeared him, but only for a minute. Her ire quickly returned

when he pushed and shoved and forced her to stand beside the
MacGreagor in front of the priest.

When her husband first arrived in their village, he claimed to be a
laird. She was not impressed but her father was. Thus set in motion the
worst day of her life. The MacGreagor let himself be tricked or
perhaps bribed, and quite easily so, into marrying her and she was
certain he had lost his wits. Of course, a man cannot lose his wits... if
he had none to begin with. That was it, she decided from the very
beginning – he was witless. Of all the husbands she might have had,
she was destined to be married to the most simple-minded one of them
all. The likelihood that she was right caused a sinking feeling to grip
her very soul. The six unusually tall, stout men the MacGreagor
brought with him said not one word the whole time they were in the
village, and even now they did not speak. Apparently, they were even
less intelligent than he...if such were possible.

It was her own fault, she knew. Laird Bisset often complained of
finding his daughter's obstinance unmanageable. Of a truth, she was
only obstinate on one subject – she refused to take a husband. On all
other subjects, she was in complete agreement with him. It was his
wife who was truly obstinate, particularly where Donaldina was
concerned. Although no one said, it was quite clear her stepmother
was behind all the marriage proposals.

Donaldina thought about the sadness on her father's face when
last she saw him. There was never a doubt that he loved her and in fact
favored her above all his other children, but how could he so easily rid

himself of her? She wished to stay with him forever, for his love was the only love she ever knew.

Abruptly, Donaldina pulled her knee up. The folds of the dreadful gown got in the way, but at last she was able to verify that the coin was still hanging from the strap around her ankle. She put her leg back down and then began to wonder whose gown it was. She had certainly never seen it before, and it was not new, but it fit her perfectly.

She was still lost in her thoughts when Wallace softly whistled, and then abruptly halted his horse. His guard instantly fanned out and faced their horses away to see to his safety. It might have been quite impressive, had she not been so furious. Instead, she rolled her eyes and again turned her face away from her husband.

"Did you not hear me?" Wallace asked. "Ye are free to go." He pulled her horse forward and handed over the reins. The expression on the face of the man with light hair and blue eyes was unmistakably determined. "But know this. If you go, do not think you can return to me."

"Do you not know you have been tricked?" she shot back. He did not answer, so she continued, "You need not take your foolishness out on me."

"Foolishness, is it? Am I not honor-bound to see to the needs of my people, no matter the insults I must endure?"

Donaldina was horrified. "You consider marriage to me an insult?"

"You hardly give me cause to consider it otherwise."

"I see." Her sarcasm was back with renewed vigor. "I am to be pleasing and appear ever so grateful to be the wife of such a glorious and wondrous lad." Her glare was as harsh as his, which she held for a very long time. At length, and because he would not look away, she was forced to. "I am not an insult to the many lads who asked for me."

"Did your father trick them as well?"

All along, she suspected one or two might have been tricked, either with ill-placed wagers or the promise of free spices, but surely not all of them. It was possible he had, she supposed, but it was easier to believe her stepmother bribed them. No matter the cause, she was not about to let this simpleton think any of the men found her undesirable. "They dinna need tricking."

"They asked for you willingly? I find that hard to believe. Why did you not marry one of them?"

The MacGreagor's sickening grin made her rage increase. "I dinna love any of them."

"How very fortunate for them!"

She gave him the sternest look she could muster. "Touch me, MacGreagor, and you die."

He leaned a little closer and looked her in the eye. "I have no desire to touch you."

She wasn't expecting that, for she had heard many an account of the brutality of men toward their wives, particularly those who thought themselves second only to God. No doubt the MacGreagor laird was one such man, for he could command his men with the slightest of nods. She might have found that impressive too, had she not felt so slighted. No desire to touch her, indeed.

"If I am free, then I shall have back my weapons," said she.

"Nay, you shall not have them."

"Why?"

"Once married, all a lass owns belongs to her husband."

Donaldina knew that was true, decided to forget about the weapons and instead looked for a place to make her way between the guards. To her chagrin, there were no openings. She did notice, however, and found it most appropriate, that the rumps of all the horses faced her husband. She might have laughed, but he was still glaring at her.

"Shall you stay or shall you go?" he demanded.

She mockingly put a thoughtful finger to her temple. "I have not yet decided."

Young Wallace MacGreagor softly whistled to get them moving again, and mumbled something in a language she could not understand. Instantly, his guards moved back in place, and this time, instead of riding beside her, he rode in front of her.

If she could have seen the faces of the two guards in front or bothered to look at the four men behind her, she would have seen all but one of them smiling. Her husband had just called her a stubborn mule in the language of the Norsemen. Hani was the guard that did not smile, but then, he never smiled.

How dare they speak a foreign language in her presence? Never had she been so insulted. She might have been further outraged by her husband's reluctance to ride beside her, but that pleased her. She was already sick of dealing with him.

At length, she bowed her head in shame. It was true, her husband had good reason to marry her, but why, oh why, had she agreed to marry him?

*

Donaldina regretted not admitting she was cold for her arms and hands were freezing. "How far must we travel?" she asked louder than was necessary.

The MacGreagor paused his horse and waited for her to catch up. "Lower your voice. Half the world can hear you and 'tis not safe."

"Did I not just hear you say, you cared not what I do?"

"I care when it endangers us, and so should you." He rode beside her in silence for a time and then answered her question before she loudly asked it again. "Our home is in the north."

Donaldina could not believe it. It was a simple question that required considerably more than a stupid answer. Of course it was in the north, or they would not be going that direction. There was nothing to do but to ask again, and speak slowly, so even he could understand. "How…far?"

"A few days."

Dismayed, she studied the side of his face. Apparently, even speaking slowly did not elicit a precise answered from him. It was useless and there was no doubt left in her mind – she was to endure such useless answers for the rest of her life. It was her father's fault. She was perfectly content to remain unmarried until the right man came along. The right man was one of knowledge and intelligence. Kindness was important too, but not as important as being able to carry on a reasonable conversation.

"Five days, perhaps six," said one of the men behind her.

Donaldina looked back and nodded her appreciation. At least one of them was sensible. "Have you a name?"

"I am Obbi," said the youngest of the Viking brothers.

"And the others?" she asked.

"I am Magnus," said one of the men in front as he raised his hand. "This is my brother, Nikolas."

"I am pleased to meet you," she said, trying as best she could to mind her manners.

"Not that pleased, I wager," said Obbi. His comment made even Hani crack a slight smile.

"I confess," she said, "I can think of a thousand places I would rather be just now."

"As can I," her husband muttered.

"Why does a Scottish lass wear the clothing of an English?" another of the guards wanted to know.

"You are?" she asked before she answered his question.

"I am Hani's favorite brother, Almoor," he answered.

"His favorite?" asked Obbi. "I thought he favored me and not you."

"You are mistaken," Almoor shot back. "You are always mistaken."

"Who is Hani?" she asked.

"I am Hani," said the guard riding beside Obbi, "and I favor neither of them. My brother Karr is my favorite."

Confused, she asked, "Which one is Karr?"

"He stayed home," Magnus answered.

There was another one, the one who captured her and put her on her horse, who rudely had not introduced himself. She cared not what his name was anyway. "Are all of you brothers?"

"Not all," her husband answered.

When that was the full extent of his answer, she drew in an exhausted breath. That his men were willing to obey such a dimwit was beyond comprehension. Conversely, his men seemed somewhat enjoyable, and at least her husband had not objected to their chatter. Perhaps he could not object. That must be it. In public they obeyed, but in private they thought little of him.

"We six are brothers, he is not," Obbi offered in answer to her question.

She turned to look back, and sure enough there were similarities in the appearance of all four. Each had blond hair, blue eyes and was about the same size…which was bigger than any other men she had ever seen. Her husband was unusually tall too, and not completely unsightly…not that she had actually looked at him in that way, nor was she ever likely to. Since Wallace had somewhat darker hair, she thought she could guess but asked anyway. "Which one is not?"

"Your husband," Obbi answered. "He is the eldest son of Laird Stefan MacGreagor. We are the grandsons of Anundi."

Donaldina lifted her right leg over the neck of her horse, scooted back a little and comfortably rode sideways so she could talk to the men behind her. "And your father?" she asked.

Obbi looked to Hani and waited for his older brother's nod before he answered. "Our father is buried in the land of the Saxons. He was a Viking."

She caught her breath and her eyes shot wide open. "A…Viking?"

"You fear Vikings?" Obbi asked.

"Of course I do, everyone does. Vikings are vicious dogs that burn our villages, kill our lads and steal our lasses. They are big, exceedingly terrible, and…" Donaldina took another look at the four men behind her, only this time she scrutinized the looks of them far more carefully. Next, she looked at the large, strong backs of the two in front and then at her husband. At length, she looked back at Obbi and slowly shook her head. "You are not…you cannae be…" Both her eyebrows shot up when he nodded.

Just in time, Wallace reached over and took ahold of her horse's halter.

That didn't stop Donaldina. She gathered her skirt, jumped off her horse, darted around the back of it, and started to run.

Reluctantly, Wallace raised his hand to stop them. The heads of all the men turned to watch her try to escape in a land so flat she could be seen for more than a mile. The back of her skirt kept catching on the heather, causing her to constantly stop, turn around, and unhook it.

Amazed, Hani said, "She runs the wrong way."

Wallace nodded. "'Tis likely she has no sense of direction."

Obbi patted the side of his horse's neck. "She cares not where she runs, for she thinks she has married a Viking."

"You are not a Viking," Almoor scoffed, "you are just the son of one."

"And the grandson of one," Wallace said.

"I pity the Viking that married her," said Steinn.

"As do I," Wallace muttered. "As do I."

Obbi frowned. "Well, I favor her."

"You favor everyone," said Hani.

"I dinna favor you for years and years," Obbi said.

Steinn was the quiet one when they first landed in Scotland, but now that he was married and more comfortable with the MacGreagors he had much more to say. "She is stupid."

"Aye, she is," Wallace agreed as he watched her stop and finally turn around to look at them. "What say you? Shall we pretend to leave without her, or simply wait until she comes back?"

"You told her not to come back," Nikolas reminded his laird. It was Nikolas who loved the stars most and expertly used them to navigate the North Sea when the brothers sailed in a stolen Viking ship. On land, there was no a need, but he still spent hours at night studying their positions.

Wallace took his eyes off his wife long enough to scan the area for danger. "Yet, if I give in now, she shall come to expect it."

"You have little choice," said Hani. "Can you not think of another way to punish her?"

"Make her ride beside Steinn," Nikolas suggested. "He thinks her stupid."

"She can ride beside me," said Obbi.

"Very well, she shall ride with Obbi," said Wallace. "I shall have nothing more to say to her." When he nodded, Obbi began to slowly walk his horse toward her.

Donaldina never imagined she would be, but she was relieved to see one of them coming for her. In her sudden impulse to run, she forgot she had no weapons, and she certainly was not willing to walk all the way back to her father's village. She had not given up her plan to escape, but now was clearly not the time.

Obbi took his time approaching her so she would not be frightened. As soon as he arrived, he halted his horse, leaned down, waited until she wrapped her arms around his neck, and then pulled her up into his lap. "You are to ride beside me, and not with your husband,"

"Are you truly Vikings?"

"Nay, we are but the sons of Vikings," he answered, as he turned his horse around. They were almost to the men when he spotted a gray wolf sitting in the tall grass a short distance away. Obbi halted and pointed to alert the men.

Donaldina did not intend to say a word. Everyone knew it was forbidden to befriend a gray wolf. Of course, that was far from the only rule she had ever broken. When her husband and two of his guards loaded their bows and pointed their arrows at the wolf, she puffed her cheeks. "Dinna shoot, 'tis only hungry."

"Do you see the pack, lads?" Wallace asked.

Each of them took a long look around before Nikolas answered, "I see nothing and I have yet to see a wolf without a pack. They lay in wait somewhere."

Steinn nodded. "Aye."

Her husband was watching her and she was well aware that any other woman would be fearful that the wolf might spook her horse or attack her in the night, yet she had already asked them not to shoot. He was clearly suspicious and all she could do was lower her gaze and continue to seem unnaturally indifferent. At last, he put his arrow back in the sheath and looped the bow string over his shoulder. Next, he lifted his hand and motioned for them to move forward.

With Obbi's help, Donaldina moved off his horse and onto hers. Her husband was not a patient man, she decided, for he had no intention of waiting until she was ready. Then again, he did let her come back, a kindness she might have appreciated, were she any other sort of woman – the sort happy to be his wife. Half of her heavy skirt was tucked under her this time, and she found the extra padding most helpful. Perhaps English women were on to something after all.

Just as they had before, Magnus and Nikolas took the lead followed by her husband and Steinn. She rode beside Obbi, while Almoor and Hani brought up the rear. Her husband's refusal to ride beside her was his way of showing his disapproval of her behavior, she knew, but she was happier where she was anyway. As hard as she tried not to, she could not resist looking back, and sure enough the wolf was following. Each time she looked back, so did Obbi, Almoor and Hani. Not once did her husband look back to see if his wife or even the wolf was following.

"'Tis your wolf?" Obbi asked at length.

Donaldina nervously giggled. "Mine? Wolves are too wild to befriend."

"Why?" Almoor asked. "'Tis just a dog."

It was not a subject Donaldina wished to discuss, so she did not answer. Eventually, the tops of the trees began to appear on the horizon. She was relieved. Each step the horses took brought them closer to a forest in which she could more easily escape…once she got her weapons back.

Most of Scotland was forest and this forest was her particular favorite, having gone hunting with her father in it each year. Birch, pine, oak, and juniper trees often grew within reach of each other, and the ground was normally carpeted in layers of moss, liverworts, and bluebells. In spring, the forest yielded wild strawberries and raspberries. More than the wildlife and the food there for the taking, she loved how the forest echoed the songs of the warblers and the hooting of the owls.

"We shall rest once we are…" Wallace started.

*

The front guards abruptly halted, causing all of them to stop, and watch as two men nonchalantly walked their horses out of the forest. Instinctively, Wallace put his hand on the handle of his sword and waited for his men to surround him and his wife.

The swiftness of their movements surprised Donaldina's horse and caused the mare to become anxious. She leaned forward and spoke softly to comfort it. As soon as her horse settled down and she managed to sit back up, her truly awful day had just gotten worse. She recognized both of the men, closed her eyes, and let her head fall forward.

It was Hani who noticed her distress, and although he did not question her, he moved his horse closer so he could pull her over to his horse if need be.

The strangers seemed placid enough as they continued toward the MacGreagors and then stopped. Their faces held no hint of their intentions, either good or bad. "We have news of a Viking raid," the first said.

"Where?" Wallace asked.

"We know not the name of the clan, only that 'tis a small village on the coast."

Wallace was relieved to know that it was neither of their neighbors, for both were large clans that often fought side-by-side when the Viking's attacked. "How long ago?"

"Three days." It was then the man spotted her. "Donaldina," said he with a grin, "your stepmother has finally cast you off, I see."

She slowly raised her eyes to meet his. "Your wife has not yet put a knife in your back, I see."

The stranger chuckled. "Nay, my wife loves me."

"I cannae imagine it," she muttered.

The stranger looked at each of the MacGreagor men trying to determine which held the highest position. He could not tell, so he chose to speak to Steinn. "I shall be happy to take her off your hands...for a fair price?"

Without hesitation Steinn asked, "How much?" When he heard Wallace clear his throat, he puffed his cheeks and moved his horse away.

The stranger turned to Wallace. "Forgive my..."

"She cannae be had for any price," the MacGreagor laird firmly said.

"Not for any price?" the confused stranger asked. Slowly and decisively, he looked from Wallace to a slumped over Donaldina and back again. "How long have you had her?"

"From sunup today," Obbi volunteered.

"Then she has not yet had time. She is shrewd and prone to…"

Wallace was not pleased. "Hold your tongue, lad."

"Hold my…" The stranger looked even more perplexed, and then the light of recognition made his eyes sparkle. "Laird Bisset has finally done it. He has tricked a lad into marrying her."

Wallace took a deep exasperated breath, raised his hand, and motioned them forward. Behind him, the two men began to chuckle and before long their chuckles became roars of laughter. Wallace ignored them and kept going.

CHAPTER 3

It took Mairi longer than she hoped to catch her horse, mount it and ride out to follow the MacGreagors. She wore a bulky masculine sheepskin cloak with a fur trimmed hood, in an effort to hide her gender from strangers. The fur helped cover her scared face as well. She was about to come out of the last clump of trees atop a small hill, when the MacGreagors suddenly stopped in the glen and the guards took up defensive positions. She could see no obvious threat, but that didn't mean there weren't any, so she found a place to hide among the trees.

When they started to move again, Mairi was again set to leave her hiding place and try to catch up. Just then, Donaldina abruptly slid off her horse and ran. Mairi prayed Donaldina's husband would leave her there, and if he did, she would happily go to the rescue. Young Mairi Bisset feared death the same as anyone, but being there when Donaldina confronted her father, would be worth the dying. After all, the scar on her face gave her little hope of securing her own happy marriage.

Unfortunately, one of the MacGreagors rode out to get Donaldina, put her on his horse and took her back. Mairi's attention was then drawn to two riders coming out of the forest, no doubt heading for the Bisset village. She saw them stop, talk to the MacGreagors, and then heard them roar with laughter. She too recognized the men as frequent visitors to the village, and had no desire to let them see her. Therefore, she had no choice but to begrudgingly stay in her hiding place and watch as the MacGreagors disappeared into the forest.

*

Donaldina looked back. Fortunately, the wolf was nowhere in sight, and the cause for her latest humiliation was about to enter the clump of trees behind them. Apparently it was true, and the whole world knew it but her – her beloved father had been tricking men into marrying her. Would a man marry just for extra salt and spices? Certainly not a man of any repute, for spices lasted less than a year and marriage was forever. Someday, she would ask her husband how it was done, but just now she did not want to know. Never would she forgive her father, even though she already missed him.

"What did he mean?" Obbi asked. She ignored him, but he would not be so easily put off. "The lad said you have not yet had time. Time for what?"

"Pay him no mind," she answered. "He is but a bitter lad."

Behind her, Hani asked, "Why is he bitter?"

"I refused to marry him. He lately married another from our clan, and I am glad of it." To end that discussion, she quickly asked a question of her own. "What do the MacGreagors do?"

"Do?" Obbi asked.

"I mean, do you farm, raise sheep, build ships…what do you do?"

Obbi chuckled. "We do what Wallace tells us to do. If he said to build a ship, we would."

In disbelief, she stared at Obbi until Hani said, "We fish, hunt, milk cows and grow food the same as any other clan. What we cannae grow, we buy"

"But not sheep?" Donaldina asked.

"Aye, we have a few sheep too for the wool. Our flock is small just now, but it is growing," Hani answered.

Nikolas nodded. "Three years past, storms wiped out our crops, drowned most of our chickens, and scattered our livestock, but the last few years have been plentiful. Even in the good years, some herbs do not grow well in the north."

"So you come to buy them from my father?"

"Aye," two of the brothers said at once.

Her husband, Donaldina noticed, said nothing which was just fine with her. "You barter with your belts?"

"Aye, we make belts," Almoor answered. "Stefan, father to Wallace, taught us how. He learned as a boy in the land of the Vikings."

"Which spices did you buy?" she asked.

"Salt crystals, naturally," Obbi answered. "We were pleased to barter for cinnamon, pepper, cloves, nutmeg, and ginger."

"My father had no saffron to sell?"

"We had no more belts," Obbi answered. Immediately, he looked back at the frown on Hani's face.

"Yet my father gave you saffron, am I right?" Donaldina asked. Her answer was no answer from any of them. "I see, taking me is barter for saffron." She glanced at the cringe on Obbi's face and felt bad for him. "Do you know where saffron comes from?"

"Nay," he answered.

"The Scots get it from the English, who get it from the French. It is very expensive. Therefore, at least I am barter for the most valuable spice of them all." It did not seem to relieve the distress in Obbi's expression, but it was the best she could do. Perhaps a man would marry for a year's worth of spices…if he was completely witless, and she was becoming more and more convinced it was an adequate description of her very own husband.

*

Mairi held her breath as the two men kept coming and then passed by without noticing her. She had lost valuable time. As soon as she dared, she looked behind her, saw no one, guided her horse back to the road, and then raced after the MacGreagors.

*

They were not long inside the thick forest when Wallace said, "Magnus." In front of him, his guard turned on his horse to see what his laird wanted. "Take us into the woods."

"Aye," Magnus answered.

Donaldina could have told them which way to go to find an animal path that ran beside a small stream, but her husband stupidly did not ask. The other direction offered steeper terrain and thicker undergrowth. Fortunately, Magnus went the right direction, so she was not put upon to correct him.

Deeper and deeper they went into the forest until they found the path and once again turned north. A short time later, Wallace stopped them and dismounted. While he adjusted the pouches of spice jars on either side of his horse, he nodded for Obbi to help her down. Shortly thereafter, he saw her walk up the path and go out of sight. Obbi looked concerned, but Wallace shook his head.

As she walked beside the small stream, the songs of the warblers and the hooting of the owls made her feel a little better. Setting aside the marriage predicament and all that went with it, she found herself enjoying more lively conversation than she had in years. Obbi liked her, of that she was certain, and although he never smiled, Hani seemed the most determined to keep her safe. She did not know if that was because she was Wallace's wife, or if he had begun to like her as well. Having friends was something she had always coveted, and for her, being accepted was a new and exciting experience. She cared nothing for her husband's opinion of her, but she had begun to worry. Instead of her making Wallace's life miserable, he had the power to make hers even more so. Perhaps, she best be kinder to her husband, if for no reason other than to avoid being isolated in her new home the way she had been in her old.

Donaldina paused, admired the late bloom on a tall bush, and then turned to go back. She had just gotten to the others when she spotted Steinn. His mouth was open and he was about to eat a mushroom. Horrified, she slapped it out of his hand. Her reward was frightening rage in Steinn's eyes, and when he took a step toward her, she stepped back, tripped over an unseen log, and started to plunge backwards. Just in time, the strong arms of a man caught her around her waist and stopped her fall.

"'Tis poison," she told Steinn in her defense. It took a moment, but as soon as Steinn understood, he softened his expression and nodded his appreciation. When she glanced back, she realized she was in the arms of none other than her husband. "Thank you," she said a little less enthusiastically than she should have. The moment she got her balance, she pushed his arms away and moved out of reach. "You must wash it off your hands," she told the men, "lest it poison your other food.

"Are all the mushrooms poison?" Obbi asked, dropping the one he had in his hand.

Donaldina was amazed. "How is it you dinna know 'twas poison?" When none of them answered, she looked at Steinn. "How long have you been in Scotland?"

"These five years," Steinn answered, "but we have yet to see mushrooms like these."

She repeatedly nodded her head. "Because you are Vikings."

"We are not. We are but the sons of a Viking," Nikolas corrected.

She didn't believe a word of it. "I see not the difference."

Obbi took a deep breath. "Have we burned your village, killed your lads and carried off your lasses?"

"Nay, but…"

Wallace forgot his vow not to speak to her. "Have we harmed you in any way?"

She turned her glare on him. "You have married me, is that not harmful enough?"

"And you have married me. We shall see which of us has been harmed the most." Disgusted, he mumbled something in the language of his father and started to walk into the forest. Abruptly, he turned back. "Furthermore, I care never to hear another word about Vikings!" He stomped off and as quickly as they could, Steinn and Hani hurried after him.

Obbi shrugged and then knelt down to wash his hands in the stream. He got up, wiped his hands on his tunic, and then asked, "Why do you wear the clothing of an English?"

"My father has many tricks," she answered as she went to Almoor's horse and started to untie her sack of belongings. "He says one thing, but he means another. He said 'twas to keep any other Scot from taking me, but 'tis a color easily spotted should I manage to run off."

"Do you mean to run off?" Nikolas asked, as he too bent down to wash his hands.

Before she could answer, Almoor said, "We shall move again soon and Wallace will not wait for any of us."

"In a hurry, is he?" she asked.

"Aye," Nikolas answered. He untied one of the smaller pouches on his horse and then used it as a counterbalance so she could have her sack of belongings on her own horse.

He failed to elaborate, and this time she did not find it insulting. "Have you nothing to eat?"

"Obbi untied a small pouch he had hanging from his belt, pulled the draw strings apart, poured a few morsels in his hand, and gave them to her. "Dried pears."

She smiled and put one in her mouth. It was sweet and chewy. "Thank you, but you dinna bring…"

"We have much more," said Almoor. He lifted a flap on one of the pouches, pulled out a fresh loaf of bread and broke off an end for her. "Your mother was more than generous."

"My stepmother, you mean. No doubt she was generous to make certain you do not bring me back out of hunger." She accepted the bread and took a bite.

Obbi grinned. "She has succeeded."

With her mouth full, Donaldina gave her first real smile to him. While she finished eating the bread, she decided it was warm enough and didn't need anything out of her sack after all. Instead, she handed it to Almoor so he could attach it to the leather strap across her horse's back. "We might be able to find some raspberries, though 'tis plenty late in the season." She tossed the rest of the dried pears in her mouth and ate them. Next, she went to the stream and knelt down. Donaldina washed her hands, and then splashed the cool, refreshing water on her face. She cupped her hands, dipped them in the water, and then drank her fill.

*

In the forest, Wallace took several deep breaths to get his irritation under control.

Still speaking the language of his homeland, Steinn said, "She dinna have to tell us 'twas poison. I might well be dead, had she not."

"We all might be," said Hani. "I wonder why. She says she wants to go home and she easily could have with the lot of us dead and dying."

Wallace shrugged and started back. "Perhaps she does not hate us as much as she claims."

"Perhaps she is not as stupid as we think either," Steinn muttered.

"You favor her?" Hani asked as he followed his brother through the bushes.

"I dinna say that," Steinn answered. "The lad cautioned us, dinna forget. He said she has not yet had time."

"Time for what, I wonder," said Hani.

Wallace frowned. "I suspect we shall find out soon enough."

*

Mairi sat on her horse in the middle of the road and tried to decide what to do. Although there were hoof prints in the dirt, none of them looked fresh except the ones created by the two men going in the opposite direction. Furthermore, the road was straight and she should have been able to see them by now. Rarely had she been away from the village, and could not guess which way to go, so she did the only thing she could do.

She shouted, "DONALDINA!"

No sooner had she shouted, than Mairi felt an arrow enter her back. She caught her breath, widened her eyes, and involuntarily arched her back. Slowly, she slumped, leaned to the side, and then fell off her horse.

Seated on his stallion, Nathair watched for a time until he was certain she was dead. Convinced he had accomplished his mission and would soon be second in command over the Bisset clan, he put his bow string back over his shoulder, turned his horse around, and went to tell his sister.

*

Standing near her horse, Donaldina thought she heard a woman call her name. She spun around just in time to see Wallace and Steinn draw their swords. Soon, the other men did as well. Her name seemed to endlessly echo through the forest, making it impossible to tell from where it came. She might have thought it her imagination, but the men had heard it too. She cupped her hands beside her mouth and started to answer, but her husband shook his head.

"Tis a trap," Steinn whispered as he drew closer to protect her.

The men waited and watched, but there were no further shouts in the forest, and when Wallace nodded, the men began to mount up. Confused by the shout in the forest, Donaldina's movements were too slow to suit her husband. Wallace took hold of her arm, turned her until she faced him, laced his fingers together to make a stirrup, and as soon as she put her foot in, he hoisted her up. He paused to make certain she was settled, mounted and then followed Magnus and Almoor on up the path. He looked back to make certain she was coming and when she gave him her usual frown, he turned his face away and smiled.

Single file, they continued to follow the animal path that took them deeper into the safety of the forest. More often than not, each of them was forced to move a tree limb out of the way. Donaldina rode behind Obbi, who was careful not to let go of a branch until he was certain she was ready to catch it, for which she was grateful. The last thing she needed was to be knocked off her horse.

None of the men were talking, so Donaldina saw no point in it either. She was obsessed with the voice that called her name anyway. It was the voice of a woman, but try as she might, she could not put a face or name to it. Her attempt at discerning it was useless, so she turned her thoughts to other things. Already tired, the realization of being on a horse for five or six days more was daunting. Yet, she still found pleasure in the warbler's songs and in admiring the delicate forest flowers. When she looked up and spotted an owl in a tree, she envied it. If only she were an owl looking down upon them instead of being one of them. Then, she could simply fly away. The truth be told, she knew she could not go home, for leaving her husband would shame her father. She was still furious with him, but she loved him too much to shame him.

As for her husband, nothing so far had convinced her that he was any sort of kind, reliable man, although he did keep her from falling over the log. Any man would have done as much…he just happened to be there. He had not even thanked her for saving the lives of his men, as surely she had. She had seen what the mushrooms could do before and it was not a pleasant sight. They might not have died, all of them, but they would have been sick enough to pray for death. Oh well, what did she care that her husband had not the good graces to thank her? The less he had to say to her the better.

*

In the bushes, the wolf watched the woman fall off her horse. It waited until the man rode away, and then crawled on its belly to Mairi. It whined as if it knew she was hurt and tried to lick her face, but Mairi pushed it away. So the wolf lay down beside her and waited. When he heard a rider coming in the far distance, he hopped up, disappeared back into the forest, hid behind a bush, and watched.

Conall MacTavish was normally a happy, carefree man. He had a wife who loved him, six children he adored and he rarely had to do the kind of hard labor put upon the backs of other men. It was for exactly that reason that he had a round belly instead of a flat one. As well, he wore a beard that exactly matched his red hair. It was cut straight across on the bottom, which made his face look strangely square.

His was an unusual gift few other men possessed. His mind was capable of remembering all faces, every name, and every word precisely the way it was said to him. Therefore, Laird MacTavish often sent Conall to one clan or another with a message, or a question that needed a detailed and accurate answer. On this day, he was on his way to ask Laird Bisset a very important question. It looked like rain, so he was eager to get to his destination.

Rarely did Conall fear an attack, for everyone in that part of the land knew and liked him. Still, he too heard a woman shout Donaldina's name and stopped to listen. It was a voice he did not recognize, which was unusual for him. He first wondered what Donaldina was doing in the forest and more importantly, was she with her father. Finding Laird Bisset in a dense forest could be done, but not easily. He listened a few minutes more for Donaldina's reply, and when there were no other shouts, he shrugged and decided to continue on. The only way to find out if Laird Bisset was away from home was to go to his castle.

It was when he rounded a bend that he saw her. In the distance someone lay unmoving in the road and considering the person's size, he suspected it was a woman. As he drew closer, he could clearly see an arrow in the victim's back and alertly scanned the area for the attacker. He saw no one, so he sped up and as soon as he reached her, he swung down off his horse. The woman lay on her side, and when he pushed the hood away from her face, he knew immediately who it was. "Mairi?"

Her eyes fluttered open and in a raspy voice, she whispered, "Donaldina."

He knelt down and then gently lifted her head. Just then, Mairi tightly grabbed hold of his sleeve. "Tell Donaldina…"

"Tell her what?"

"Her mother dinna die...Basset sent her away."

Conall was astonished. "Why did he send her away?"

Mairi gasped for her next breath. "The twin had dark hair."

He let his held breath escape in a whistle. "Where is Donaldina?"

Her speech became more and more labored, and there was less strength in her grip. "Married off," she whispered.

Conall glanced into the forest, realized it was likely too late to find Donaldina, and turned his attention back to the dying woman. "Mairi, you must rest now."

"She..."

"Hush now. I shall take you home." He was too late. The muscles in her face relaxed, she let go of his sleeve and her hand fell away. Mairi's eyes turned black...the same as all eyes did in death, and Conall knew all hope was lost. He slowly stood up and made the sign of the cross over her.

Some men boldly marked the shaft of their arrows, and such was the case of the one sticking out of Mairi's back. The owner had carved a small half-moon in it, and Conall recognized it immediately. He considered pulling the arrow out and tossing it away, but thought better of it.

"Let Laird Bisset do what he will about the murder of a member of his clan," said he.

A few feet away, her horse was feasting on a patch of green grass. Cautiously, he approached it, grabbed hold of the reins, and then brought it back to the road. As reverently as was possible without disturbing the arrow, he put Mairi's body face down over her horse, mounted his, and took her home.

The wolf watched the man take Mairi away, and then scurried through the bushes.

*

It began as just a slight breeze that made the leaves in the tress flutter. Being so deep in the forest, Donaldina was only able to catch an occasional glimpse of the storm clouds gathering overhead. As everyone knew, horses considered a strong wind a sign of danger. To them, movement in the trees and bushes meant predators were on the attack. Her horse was no different, and as the wind speed increased, the mare began to dance from one side of the path to the other, trying to avoid the moving bushes. As well, loose leaves and twigs started to sail through the air, which served to spook the horses that much more.

Behind her, Hani watched as she leaned forward, stroked the animal's neck, and began to talk to the horse in hushed tones. In response, the horse's ears perked up and the mare started to calm. Hani had never seen a woman do that before. In fact, he had never seen a man do it either. Following her example, he did the same and found his horse equally responsive.

Spooked horses were not their only concern, and Wallace looked back often to check on his wife and his men. When he could no longer see her, he halted his horse and started to go back. That caused her to rise up to see what was amiss, and he breathed a sigh of relief. He was about to keep going when he heard her yell over the noise of the wind.

"At the next fork, turn right."

Wallace frowned. He was hardly inclined to let a woman tell him what to do, even if she was his wife. Yet, when they came to a place where the animal path split, the guards in front of him turned right and he said nothing. A few minutes later, they entered a fairly large clearing and stopped. It was just in time, for the dark clouds had begun to yield their droplets of water.

As quickly as they could, the men untied the spice pouches and placed them near the trunk of a lush oak tree to keep them from getting wet. Although the spices were in tightly sealed leather jars, the lids were made of cloth and letting them get wet would be a disaster. Even though the ground beneath them stayed dryer, oak trees were the most dangerous. The thickness of the leaves sometimes became a canopy that allowed a strong wind to uproot a tree if the ground became too rain soaked. Hopefully, that would not happen.

Donaldina slid off her horse, pulled her sack and the counterweight off, and when she turned around, Wallace was standing right behind her. She lightly shoved him away, and instead went to stand in front of the mare. She petted the horse's nose and kept talking to her thousand pound best friend, but this time she wasn't getting it calmed down. She knew Wallace was yelling at her to let go of the halter, but she ignored him. The wind howled and the trees bent back and forth, but it was not until a limb broke and nearly hit her in the head, that she completely lost control of her horse. She jumped out of the way and watched as the mare joined the other horses in their repeated race around the clearing.

Wallace stood with his arms folded frowning at her, but she was not intimidated. She rolled her eyes, skirted around him and went to stand under the same tree as Obbi. Abruptly, her husband grabbed her arm. "I will go with Obbi," she protested.

"'Tis forbidden," he shouted. Wallace pulled her to the trunk of another tree, took off his cloak, lifted it up, and held it over both their heads.

"Why 'tis forbidden?"

"Because you are my wife."

"I may be your wife, but I am not your possession."

"'Tis the same thing."

Despite the rain drops running off the tip of her nose, she still managed to glare at him. "'Tis not the same thing. Your horse, your cottage, and your clan may be your possession, but I am not."

"'Tis not a cottage, 'tis a castle."

Too dumbfounded to have a ready response, Donaldina pulled the sleeve of her gown down, wiped the excess water off her face, and then looped her sack string over her shoulder. The leather pouch counterbalance on the other end of the strap fell to the ground, but she did not care. Everyone knew that only Scots with vast holdings had castles, save for the king, and Wallace MacGreagor certainly was not the king. At any rate, he managed to change the subject and she was not about to let him get away with it. "Do you admit that a wife is not a husband's possession?"

"I do not."

Furious, she turned her back to him. It made Wallace smile. Harsh gusts of howling wind threatened to tear the cloak out of his hands and drove the rain sideways, getting both of them wet. Had she been a little more appreciative, he might have drawn her close and wrapped his cloak tightly around her to keep her dry. As it was, she kept busy trying to keep the wind from lifting her English skirt.

At length, the wind slowly subsided and the horses began to calm down. After so much excitement, they would need extra rest and grazing in the tall grass would be good for them. Besides, it was still raining. He lifted his cloak a little higher to check on his men and the pouches. Apparently, his wife was making faces and Obbi found her entertaining. Wallace sighed.

Obbi found lots of things entertaining. Of the brothers, he was the closest to Wallace's age, he was hardworking and fun to go hunting with. Most of all, Obbi had a way of seeing the world through different eyes than most. Nikolas and the other men appeared to be just as entertained. At home, Nikolas had begun to teach the children how to read the stars. More often than not, half the clan lay or sat nearby so they could learn as well. Almoor, third from the youngest of the brothers, had no particular skill when they first arrived, but once he was taught, he became the most creative when it came to making belts. As well, Almoor was good with the animals and especially loved dogs.

Standing under different trees, the oldest brothers, Magnus, Steinn, and Hani were not entertained. Instead, they stayed watchful and alert for fear thieves might take advantage of the bad weather and attack.

The wind had subsided, but the rain had not when Donaldina abruptly turned to face her husband again. "When the storm passes, I require ample time to rest."

"You are resting."

"Nay, I am not. I wish to sit down."

Wallace took a step back, leaving her plenty of room to sit beside the tree, but from the look on her face, that wasn't going to be good enough. "What?"

"Am I expected to sit at your feet like a slave?"

He raised an eyebrow. "Are you asking me to sit with you or sending me away?"

"Would you go away if I asked?"

"Nay."

"I thought not," she scoffed.

"I have but one cloak and it stays with me."

She looked down, pointed at her wet skirt and said, "I wish to change clothes."

"You would disobey your father?"

She threw up her hands and looked all around. "Where? I dinna see him here. Oh, you mean the father who happily married me off simply to win a wager?"

"A wager?" a surprised Wallace asked.

"You dinna know? You are even more…"

"More what?"

She ignored him and refused to answer.

"I believed the word you care not to say is foolish."

Irritated beyond all that was good and holy, she turned her back to him a second time. How could he possibly have missed all the merriment her clan exhibited the night before? He could not have…unless he was lying. Yet, why lie about a thing like that, she wondered. Perhaps her husband's character was even more polluted than she previously suspected. She stuck her head out from under his cloak and looked up at the sky. It was not as dark as it had been, and with any luck at all, it would soon stop raining. When it did, she could find another place to be…any place at all would do, so long as it was not beside him.

Wallace tapped her on the shoulder, which made her turn back around to see what he wanted. He asked, "How far to the next resting place?"

It was a sensible question for once, so she decided to give him a sensible answer. "We are nearly to a loch where you can fish for our dinner…if you know how to fish."

Laird Wallace MacGreagor stared into her spiteful eyes. "In our clan, the lasses do the fishing."

"What?"

"'Tis tradition. The lads hunt and the lasses fish."

She raised her voice a little. "'Tis not my tradition."

He matched the volume of her voice with his. "It is now!"

"I protest."

"And quite often," he shot back. It was all he could do to keep from chuckling, but he kept his emotions under careful regulation.

"I would rather hunt?"

"I would rather you fish. We are a hungry lot and require many fish to fill our bellies."

"I suspect you do, but you shall do it without my help." She would have stomped off, had it not been raining so hard. Instead, she thought to change the subject and ask a few questions of her own – just to see what other lies he would tell. "Are all the lads without wives?"

"Nay, all but Nikolas, Almoor and Obbi have wives."

"Which is the eldest?"

"Karr is the eldest. He is married to my sister, Catrina. Hani took a Macoran wife as did Steinn, and Magnus married a Brodie. The lads came to us as builders but have since learned other talents."

"Such as guarding you?"

"Aye and you."

She looked away. She had not truly considered what being the wife of a laird involved. Her stepmothers, the ones she could remember, demanded all sorts of privileges, but Donaldina knew not if other clans were the same. At any rate, she would gladly trade being guarded for her freedom. It occurred to her she might not be a welcome addition to the MacGreagor Clan, but then, perhaps she might manage to escape before she was faced with that dilemma. It was something to think about, anyway. "How many in your clan?"

"At last count, three hundred and three. 'Twill hopefully be three hundred and five by the time we get home."

"Tis a small clan, then."

"A small clan, perhaps, but we have pleasant neighbors, good land, and healthy children."

"And a castle?"

"A hidden castle," he corrected.

Hidden from everyone but him, she suspected. "Do your neighbors live close?"

"Aye, we were once enemies with the Brodies, but we have settled our differences. Clan Macoran and Limond live on the coast, and we have strong ties with each as well. Laird Limond of old was my father's grandfather."

"They live on the coast? Are they not attacked by the…" she caught herself before she said the forbidden word.

"Aye, they are, and we fight alongside our neighbors when need be. Vikings have yet to come inland far enough to attack us directly."

Apparently, he could say the word and she could not. Once he said not to, it became a rule and rules exasperated her, especially silly ones. At least they were having a pleasant conversation. She might have been more pleased had he not claimed to live in an imaginary castle. She lifted the edge of his cloak to see where her horse was. The mare seemed content to graze with the other horses. She stuck her hand out and at last, the rain had turned to sprinkles. Donaldina pushed her husband's cloak back, walked toward the clearing and just as she did, her horse came to her.

Donaldina lovingly patted the mare's nose. "Such a good lass are you. You're a bit wet, but we cannae help that, can we."

Behind her, Wallace watched with great interest. His horse always came when he whistled, but her horse came just at the sight of her. It pleased him very much. It was a good sign that she was kind to children and animals alike…just not husbands.

Donaldina walked a few feet away, turned her back to all the men, and tried to ring the water out of her skirt. When she had done the best she could, and looked, the men were brushing the water off the horses and getting the pouches loaded. What surprised her most was that Almoor was brushing her horse. Her mare rarely let anyone else get near it. Suddenly, the horse swished its wet tail his direction and sloshed water all over Almoor. She tried not to, but when Almoor turned his chagrinned expression her way, she laughed.

At her husband's command, the MacGreagors set out again.

There were few things Donaldina liked more than the glistening rays of sunshine when they broke through forest trees, seeing raindrops on leaves, and smelling the crisp fresh air. She forgot herself and basked in the glory of it for quite some time before she remembered. She was married to a ridicules man, and there was nothing she could do about it.

*

Conall MacTavish made it to the village before the heavy rain began. As soon as they saw him approach leading a horse with a body on it, the guards opened the gates and let him in. He walked his mare right up to the castle door and by the time he dismounted, two men were there to see whose body it was. Both were shocked to learn it was Mairi, but upstairs in the castle window, Laird Bisset's wife was not.

Conall again made the sign of the cross as the men pulled the arrow out and then carried Mairi away. After they were out of sight, he used the large, half circle clang to knock on the castle door. Almost immediately, a house servant came to let him in.

"Conall MacTavish to see Laird Bisset."

The manservant nodded and then leaned closer. "'Tis in a foul mood today."

"I see." It would not be the first time Conall had to deal with the ugly mood of a laird, but he especially hated Laird Bisset, even when he was in a good mood. The man had a reputation for swindling the northern clans...and getting away with it. As was usual, he found the object of his dislike sitting at the head of a long table in the darkened Great Hall. Conall had just walked in when a guard rushed past him. The guard laid the arrow on the table near Bisset, and then whispered in his laird's ear.

"Mairi?" Laird Bisset gasped. "What was she doing away from the village?" He suddenly caught his breath. "You dinna suppose she…"

"Ask him," said the guard nodding toward Conall. "'Twas he who brought her back."

Laird Bisset rose up out of his seat, came closer, and raised his voice. "Where was she?"

"She lay in the middle of the road."

"Yet alive?"

Conall looked the angry man straight in the eye and lied. "Nay, she was already dead when I happened upon her." Conall had the gift of remembering everything he heard, and he had another gift besides – he was wise enough not to repeat everything he heard. Besides, knowing what he knew now might benefit him sometime in the future.

Laird Bisset looked relieved, went back to his chair, and picked up the arrow. When he too recognized the mark, he whispered something to his guard, who immediately left the room. Laird Bisset frowned and then laid the arrow back down. "Did you happen to see my daughter on your way here?" he asked Conall.

"Nay, should I have?"

"Aye, she was married this morning and her husband said he was taking her north."

"Did she not pledge never to marry?"

Laird Bisset chuckled. "Aye, and often. Still, I have my ways, even where my children are concerned. If you dinna see her on the road, they must have diverted…or, they are not a northern clan as they said."

"Which clan is it? Perhaps I know them?"

"They claimed to be MacGreagors."

Conall truly had never heard of them, so he slowly shook his head. "I know not that clan."

"Well, he seems a good lad. He will treat her well."

"Then she is fortunate you have found him."

Just then, a woman servant rushed into the room, lifted the front of her skirt, and dashed up the stairs. Laird Bisset rolled his eyes. "Gone up to tell my wife about Mairi. I am always amazed at how quickly the gossip spreads in this village."

"'Tis not unlike many other villages, I assure you."

"Sit down, Lad. What have you come to tell me?"

He did as he was bid, and not a moment later he heard Mistress Bisset cry out in anguish. Laird Bisset rolled his eyes again and Conall respectfully bowed his head. There were rumors about Mairi and how her face came to be damaged. At the time, Conall thought little of it, but now that he knew Mairi's secret, a lot of rumors about the Bisset village were beginning to make sense.

"Why have you come to see me, Lad?" Laird Bisset asked a second time.

Conall raised his head and cleared his throat the way he always did when he began to recite a question. "Laird MacTavish wishes to know if you have heard rumors of an English attack."

"Attack? Why would they attack?"

"He did not confide the reason for his question."

"I see. Nay, I have heard nothing at all about the English bearing arms against the Scots, but I shall keep my ear to the ground and send word the moment I do."

Conall stood up. "Laird MacTavish can wish for nothing more." He started to leave and then though better of it. "Have you a message to send back?"

For several moments, Laird Bisset stared at the arrow and appeared to be deep in thought. At length, he waved Conall away and looked at him no more. Relieved, Conall happily walked out the door.

Once outside, Conall strolled down a village path until he saw a cottage eve wide enough to protect him from the rain. The two women inside could not have known he was there when one said, "Poor Mairi. She was the only one brave enough to say the truth, and look what has become of her."

The second woman continued kneading her batch of bread dough. "How it did break my heart each time Donaldina went to her mother's stone in the graveyard, but what could we do? We, each of us, are bound by his lies."

"Well, I say he deserves the vile wife he has now. Already she makes him miserable and I cannae think why he married her."

The first woman snickered. "She is handsome and 'tis reason enough for some lads."

Conall looked in the direction of the graveyard and considered going to see the headstone, but thought better of it lest Laird Bisset suspect he knew the truth. A ruckus in front of the castle drew his attention next. Laird Bisset's brother-in-law was being hauled through the Great Hall's doors against his will. Conall watched until the door closed, and then decided – rain or no rain, it was time to leave.

CHAPTER 4

It was early evening when Mistress Tearlag Bisset avoided the puddles of water, walked down the path between the cottages, and went to see her brother. Her marriage to Laird Bisset gained Nathair a fine cottage to live in, even though he had not yet taken a wife, and she had delighted in furnishing it with odds and ends her husband would never miss from the castle. Three large candles on the table illuminated the room, and he had just finished what he considered to be a well-deserved supper.

"Well?" she asked as she closed the door, went to the table, and sat down opposite her brother. "What did my husband want?"

"Conall brought back the arrow with my mark on it and Laird Bisset asked if I killed her."

"What did you tell him?"

"The truth."

"You confessed?" she gasped.

"And rightly so," Nathair beamed. "He is grateful for my having stopped Mairi before she could find Donaldina."

Tearlag relaxed a little. "I see. You dinna tell him I put you up to it, did you?"

"Of course not, but I thought to give you at least some of the credit. He dismissed me before I could."

"I am glad you dinna. 'Twill be less complicated this way. You are certain he is glad you killed her?"

"I am quite certain. He said neither of us would speak of it again." Nathair picked up the arrow, wet a rag with water from his cup, and began to rid it of Mairi's blood. "When do you think to suggest he make me second in command?"

She considered it for a moment, and then carefully chose her words. "Let us wait until he has had time to reconsider. In a day or two, he might not find the killing of a member of his clan so palatable." Pleased, Tearlag stood back up. "I best get back before I am missed. The old frog likes his supper just as the sun goes down and will not budge off it. 'Tis one more thing I hope to change."

*

When evening came, Donaldina was considerably more apprehensive than she had been all day. She still did not have her weapons back, which meant she could not effectively fight off a husband, particularly one as big as hers. After the spices were once more unloaded and when the men walked down to the loch, she stayed several yards from the shore with her hands on her hips. She said nothing, but dared them to force her to do the fishing. Curiously, the men made no hint that they expected her to.

Instead, Wallace followed his men to the water, took the large, gold medallion off his neck, and handed it to Nikolas. In turn, Nikolas used it to reflect the setting sun on the edge of the water. Three of the men drew their swords and got ready to spear fish that were attracted to the light. It took a moment, but soon Steinn thrust his weapon in the water and proudly withdrew the first catch of the day.

Donaldina forgot her hands were defiantly on her hips as her husband came back and walked past. She detected a slight taunting smile on his face, leaving no doubt in her mind that she had been tricked. Annoyed, she folded her arms and watched him walk to the tied horses. If she was not to fish, she wondered, what did he expect of her? Almoor and Hani were busy gathering dry moss and wood from under the trees with which to build a fire, her husband was seeing to the horses, and instead of working, she had nothing at all to do.

Wallace examined all four of the first horse's hooves, untied it, retied the reins over its neck, and sent it off to graze. The second horse had a pebble in its hind hoof, which he dug out with his dagger, and then sent it on its way too. However, when he got to her horse, it shied away from him.

Still exasperated, Donaldina walked to her horse, spoke softly as she approached and untied it. "Arwen dinna like being tied." She rubbed the mare's nose and just as he had, tied the reins over its back. "There, 'tis better now."

"Your mare is indeed a noble maiden. 'Tis a fitting name."

Donaldina didn't care if he thought it fitting or not. She kept talking to the mare while her husband checked its hooves and then said, "You may go." The mare nodded, backed up, and then casually walked away.

"You have trained her well."

"We are friends, she and I, which I cannae say for the two of us. I dinna take kindly to your lie."

"Which one?" he asked, lifting the front hoof of yet another horse.

"There is more than one?"

"I can think of several, beginning with a particular wedding vow."

She deeply wrinkled her brow. "Which vow?"

"Well, if I am not allowed to touch you for fear of death, I must seek my company elsewhere."

"You would willingly commit adultery?"

"If I am not allowed to touch my wife, I have no other choice. A Laird must have sons."

She considered that for a moment. Her nature was to argue with him, but on this subject she thought not to. "Very well, I have no objection." With that, she turned and walked away.

Wallace brushed a fly away from his face, and watched her take her sack of belongings to a log and sit down. He checked another hoof and then saw her pull her ordinary clothing out, set the sack aside and then walk into the forest. This time, both Obbi and Nikolas looked concerned, but Wallace shook his head. Instead, he continued to check hooves, repeatedly looked her direction, and then set the last of the horses free.

Donaldina tossed the damp gown into the bushes, and hurried to put on her comfortable clothes. She would have liked her hair braided a different way, but that could wait for later. When she was finished dressing, she took a moment to more carefully examine the gown. She should not have been so surprised that her father had it, for he was forever taking the oddest things as barter for the spices. Even so, it fit very well and that puzzled her. She spread the gown out across a bush and then ran her hand over the soft material. Never before had she felt anything that soft, and it really was quite beautiful. It had tablet woven, gold and white braid that trimmed the neck opening and the bottom of each of the sleeves. For a moment, she considered taking it with her, but what for? It would only remind her of the father who so easily rid himself of her. Still irked at him, she wadded up the gown and tossed it away.

When she came back, Wallace was waiting and seemed to approve of her long brown skirt, the simple white shirt she wore under a long tan vest, and the wide belt she had around her waist. When he nodded, she lifted her fluttering eyes to the sky and walked away. What she wore was incomplete as long as he kept her weapons, and he obviously didn't realize that.

It was a habit she started long ago, and without thinking, she bent down and checked to make certain the Roman coin was still on the string tied around her ankle. To her relief, it was. When she was younger, she found the coin fascinating. It had the face of a less than handsome man on one side, and two men shaking hands on the other side. She supposed she would never know what the letters meant, but it didn't matter. She had worn it for so long, she knew she would feel lost without it. She supposed her husband had seen her look at it, and wondered what it was, but it was none of his business.

Donaldina walked to the loch, knelt down, and washed her face. It was the barest of glimpses, but she caught sight of the wolf's nose sticking out from behind a bush. Her heart sank for she feared sooner or later, the men would shoot it. Furthermore, she had no food to give. Perhaps later she might slip a fish to him, but just now she was more concerned about its safety. It was best not to draw attention to it, so she walked back to the fire the men were building.

Wallace was right about one thing – it took a lot of fish to feed this hungry lot, but it seemed the men were going to catch enough. Each time a fish was speared, the owner cleaned it, brought it to the fire, wrapped it in leaves, and set it near the fire to cook. Obbi was the last to come away from the water, and as he did, he too noticed the wolf. By then, it was sitting up as if begging, and Obbi was too kind hearted to let it go hungry. On his sword were two fish, so he pulled one off, looked to be sure no one saw him, and tossed it to the wolf.

Donaldina smiled. It was a pity she had not married Obbi instead of the man on the other side of the fire – the one that was constantly watching her. When Obbi came back and sat beside her, she asked. "Has your mother passed?"

"Aye."

"Mine too. She passed when I was but four years old."

Obbi nodded, "I am the youngest and dinna recall my mother much. Mostly, Karr and grandfather cared for us."

Donaldina wrinkled her brow. "I have no grandfather. Is that not odd?"

"Many a lad dies before his grandchildren are raised up."

"Aye, but why have I never heard of my mother's father…or her mother for that matter?"

"Perhaps 'twas too painful for your father to speak of."

"That must be it," Donaldina was not quite satisfied with that answer, but she let it pass. "Just now I am reminded of how pleased I am never to have to live in the same home as my stepmother."

"You dinna like her?" Nikolas asked. The sun was nearly down, and with a stick he poked one of the fish to see how well cooked it was. Soon, all the fish would need to be turned, and when they were ready to eat, Magnus would divide up the bread Mistress Bisset sent with them. Nikolas was already licking his lips.

"Nay, and 'twas the same for her. She is my father's fifth wife and I wager he shall live long enough to have three or four more." She enjoyed the smiles on all their faces. Naturally, Hani's eyes smiled, but his mouth did not.

Just then, Nikolas remembered, took the medallion off from around his neck, and started to return it to Wallace.

"May I see it?" Donaldina asked.

When Wallace nodded, Nikolas handed it to her instead. "'Tis gold and reflects the sun."

"I saw you do that." She turned it over and looked, but there were no markings on the back.

"'Twas my grandmother's," Wallace volunteered.

"The one married to a Viking?" she asked whether her husband objected to the word or not. "'Tis stolen, no doubt."

"Nay," Wallace answered. "'Twas a gift from her father, Laird Limond of old."

"A Scot?" she asked.

"Aye," her husband answered.

Donaldina looked Wallace in the eye. "Before she was carried off by a Viking?"

Instantly put out, Wallace got up and walked into the forest. Behind him, he heard his wife say, "Dinna get lost." Before he got very far, Almoor and Steinn came to see to his safety. Steinn began to speak, but Wallace held up his hand to stop him. For several minutes he kept his back to his men, rubbed the back of his neck, and tried to think. At length, he turned around. "Suggestions?"

"She is frightened," Almoor whispered.

"What possibly makes you say that?" Wallace asked. "She dinna look frightened."

"That is just how I know. She is naysaying to hide her fear."

Wallace shook his head. "Well, she has nothing to fear from us."

"Aye, but she dinna know that," Almoor said. "Her father told you to lay a hand to her backside."

"Dinna tempt me," said Wallace as he looked up at what little of the sky he could still see. The storm clouds were nearly gone which meant the night would be cold.

"You will not harm her," Steinn scoffed, "you took the oath the same as we."

Almoor stood with his legs apart and folded his arms. "Perhaps you should tell her about the edict."

"And perhaps not," Wallace said. "Once she knows I am forbidden by the edict, I'll never get her settled down."

Steinn couldn't help but grin. "I doubt you can anyway."

Wallace took a deep breath. "I fear you might be right." The hoot of an owl made him decide to go back, and when he did, the others were sitting around the fire trying to explain how they got to Scotland. Everyone, including his wife ignored his return. The fish had been turned to cook on the other side, and Magnus was busy cutting four loaves of bread in half.

"You each came on a long ship?" Donaldina asked.

"Aye, but different ships," Hani answered.

"Why?" she asked.

The question stumped Nikolas for a moment. "Oh, I see what you are thinking. Wallace's father came years before. We seven came later."

She finally understood and then wrinkled her brow again. "If you dinna come to murder the Scots, why did you come?"

"Because…" Nikolas started.

"They came," Wallace interrupted, "So they would not have to become Vikings like their father. They are good, peaceful men, just as my father was, and I care to hear no more about Vikings." With everyone watching, he picked up his cloak and spread it out on the ground near the flickering fire. "For you," he told Donaldina, "when you are tired." He sat down, untied his flask, and took a sip of ale.

"And where are you to sleep?" she asked.

He studied the look in her eyes and considered what it might mean. "You fear me?"

She hesitated to answer, instead glancing around at all the other eyes watching her. "I would not in the slightest if you would give back my weapons."

In spite of his earlier irritation, Wallace smiled. "'Tis I who should fear you then?"

"All I ask is a fighting chance." She was serious, but each and every MacGreagor was grinning. What that meant, precisely, was something she could not even guess. Had she waited too long to run?

At last, Wallace took pity on her. "I shall sleep near you but not with you. For your protection, all of us shall sleep near you. As well, each lad shall take a turn standing guard."

She couldn't help but look at Obbi to see if her husband was lying.

Obbi reassured her with a nod. "We dinna force lasses, even our wives...should each of us finally have a wife."

"You dinna force...? My stepmother said..."

"Nay, we dinna," Wallace confirmed. "The punishment for such as that is death."

She was astounded. Her stepmother told her to expect the worst, yet her husband looked her straight in the eye and did not look away. At length, she decided she believed him. That was one huge worry off her mind. She lowered her gaze and for a long moment, stared into the diminishing fire. If she was clever enough, she might just make it through the night, escape, and never have to be in his arms…if she was clever enough. Each of the men seemed to be watching her, so she changed the subject, "Have you any brothers and sisters?" she asked her husband.

Wallace answered, "The fever took my father and all but two sisters and two brothers."

"The fever last year?" she asked. She watched as Nikolas used a forked stick to pick up one of the fish, set in a wooden bowl and then passed it to Magnus. Magnus added bread and passed the bowl to Donaldina. "Thank you," she whispered.

"Nay, three years past," Wallace answered. "Before that, we were ten children. Now we are five." The next to be served, he accepted his bowl and began to carefully peal the leaf away from the hot fish.

She felt bad for her husband. "I had neither a brother nor a sister to lose. I was my mother's only child." Donaldina looked sad for a moment.

"You have no half-brothers or sisters?" Steinn wanted to know. "If your father has had five wives, you must have some."

"Seven, at last count, but they dinna fancy me." She didn't object when sitting next to her, Almoor took her bowl. With his knife, he expertly peeled off the leaf, opened her fish, removed the bone, and handed the bowl back to her.

"None of them?" Wallace asked. "Why?"

She took a moment to yawn. "'Tis complicated."

"How complicated?" Steinn pushed.

"They claim my father favored me over any of them, for he loved my mother best."

"How did she die?" Wallace asked.

"I think she was murdered, but Father says not."

"Murdered?" Nikolas asked. "Who…"

She took a moment to blow on the hot meat. "I never discovered it…and now that I am gone, I suppose I never shall. Still, something is not quite right about what my father says. Oh, there is a stone to mark where she is buried, but…" Donaldina paused to collect her thoughts.

"But what?" Steinn asked as he watched Nikolas take two fish and a half loaf of bread, and then sit down beside him.

"But if he loved her best, why does my father not ever go there himself to mourn the loss of her?"

"And this is why you think she was murdered?" Magnus asked.

"Nay, I think it because no one will answer my questions. I wished to know all about her, but when I asked, they said to ask Father. One of the elders told me she was a handsome lass who loved my father dearly, but that is all she would say." Donaldina turned her glare once more on her husband. "I would have gone to her grave to bid my mother goodbye, had you not whisked me away like a thief."

"Do you not mean a foolish thief?" Wallace corrected.

"If you insist," she shot back.

"If you had been a willing bride, I would have allowed you to visit her grave."

"Allowed me? Be forewarned, Laird MacGreagor, I have always done, and shall continue to do, precisely as I please."

Wallace ignored the brothers who were watching to see what he would say, "And I shall allow you to." While the others chuckled, he slowly began to smile.

Donaldina wrinkled her brow. She wasn't sure if she won or lost that argument. While she contemplated which, she ate her fish and her bread.

His stomach full finally, Almoor took a stick and started to separate the last of the embers so the fire would go out. "Surely not all of your brothers and sisters refused to abide you."

She shrugged. "Children grow up believing what they are taught. They were taught to shun me. 'Tis of no account now anyway. I shall never have to abide them again either." She was quiet for a moment before she glanced around the circle of men and said, "Thank you."

Obbi looked confused. "For what?"

"For answering my questions. I am sad to hear the MacGreagors lost loved ones. The fever takes so many of the children each year, and I worry that Scotland shall never have enough stout men to fight off the…" horrified by what she was about to say, she abruptly caught her breath.

"…Vikings," Obbi said for her. He quickly looked to see if he was in trouble, but Wallace was amused.

Donaldina yawned again and when she did, the men gathered the bowls and Magnus took them to the loch to wash. Nikolas and Obbi spread their cloaks next to the one she was to sleep on, while Almoor offered his hand to help her stand up. As soon as she lay down and was wrapped up in Wallace's cloak, Almoor leaned down and playfully tucked the edges in as if she were a child. It made her smile.

*

Steinn took the first watch.

Wallace might as well have, for he could not sleep. Instead, he walked to the edge of the loch and looked out over the water. Occasionally, he looked back at his sleeping wife and then at Steinn, but he said nothing. Three of the men were snoring, but it didn't seem to be keeping Donaldina awake. At length, he motioned for Steinn to come talk to him.

"What?" Steinn asked.

Wallace pointed to the empty place where the fish had been gutted. "The wolf?"

"Aye," Steinn answered. "It follows her."

"She shall be a good mistress for our clan…someday."

"She already is."

Wallace looked again at the woman who peacefully and innocently slept. "Aye, but she hates the sight of me."

"Nay, she does not hate you. Hate is when they dinna take the trouble of talking. Hate is when your supper is cold, and…"

"Your wife vexes you?"

Steinn yawned and tried to make light of it. "Not today."

Wallace smiled. "Nor tomorrow or the next."

"Aye. God willing, she shall have got over it by then."

He put a hand on Steinn's shoulder and then went to bed.

*

Morning came far too soon.

Donaldina woke up with her husband's warm cloak wrapped around her. She lazily stretched, remembered where she was, and abruptly sat up. The men were already up, the horses had been gathered, and the pouches loaded. Even her sack was tied to her horse. How she managed to sleep through all that was a mystery to her.

She went into the forest for her relief, and when she came back, she immediately checked to make certain her coin was still there. It was. By then, her husband was waiting beside her horse. Apparently, her stepmother had included it, for he held her hooded, dark gray cape open for her, and when she turned her back, he put it over her shoulders. Any other time, she would have found his intrusion into her belongings offensive, but the morning was chilly and she needed the warmth. As soon as she finished hooking the top clasp, he lifted her up, sat her on her horse, and then waited to make certain she was awake enough to safely ride.

"I am able to mount a horse by myself," she mumbled.

"I am happy to hear that, for I might not always be with you." He handed her a small bag of dried fruit and bread, and then fetched her horse's reins for her.

"Thank you," she managed to say. He was being terribly kind, which meant he was up to something. Hopefully, she would soon be awake enough to discover what it was. He was somewhat pleasant the night before too, but she was not fooled. Most men were pleasant when they had a little ale in their bellies. Maybe that was it. Her husband enjoyed his ale in the mornings too. She made a mental note to keep an eye on his ale flask. It would be just her luck to end up married to a drunkard.

The eight of them again rode single file on a path that took them to the other side of the loch, only this time Wallace rode directly in front of her with Obbi in back. She would rather look at Obbi than her husband, but complaining was useless.

There was not a bone in her body that was not already sore, but it would do not good to complain about that either. Nevertheless, she did regret not making a cushion of sorts out of the English gown. She considered asking to go back, but how would she explain? There were other ways to compensate for a sore bottom and they would likely make several suggestions. She might say she left something in it, but what? All she had was her coin and she had not made a secret of checking for it. Oh well, she thought, too late now.

When it came time to rest, she was more than grateful and instead of waiting to be helped, she put a leg over and quickly slid down. She was also grateful when Almoor offered her a drink of water from his flask. Almoor was an interesting brother. Of the three youngest, he seemed the most shy and when he was thoughtful, which he often was, he absentmindedly chewed his lower lip. He was also the most handsome, in Donaldina's opinion, and she wondered why some young woman had not yet snatched him up.

"Why do you wear a coin on your ankle?" Almoor asked when she finished drinking and handed the flask back.

"On the ankle I am forbidden to let you see?" she asked. It embarrassed him a little, which made her smile. "'Tis another mystery. Will you walk with me?"

Almoor looked to see if Wallace approved, and then nodded. This time, the curious Obbi and the normally suspicious Steinn went with them, leaving the others to see to the horses.

They had only gone a few feet back down the path, when she stopped and put her hands on her hips. "When I was small, the lass that cared for me said 'twas my mother's. I know not if that was true. I know not a lot of things. I know not who killed my mother, I know not what she looked like, I know not where the purple gown came from, and most of all, I know not from where the coin came."

"Why do you not take it off," Steinn asked.

She considered that and started them walking again. "I have no place other to keep it safe."

"When we are home," said Obbi, "We shall make you a belt with a pocket on the inside. That will keep the coin safe."

"Is the coin of value?" Almoor asked.

"I dinna see how it could be. 'Tis made of gold possibly, but 'tis very old and unlike any other coin I have ever seen."

Steinn walked in front of them with his hand on the handle of his sword just in case they encountered danger. "To hear you tell it, 'twas not a pleasing upbringing."

"Not all of it. I had my horse and my father's love. 'Twas enough on most days…until now. Now I have been cast away like shoes with holes in the bottom."

"Not true. He chose a good husband for you," Almoor argued.

"Did he? I see." She was quiet after that and the brothers seemed to have run out of questions. When she paused to admire a flower and then a butterfly, they patiently waited. They were on their way back when she asked, "I wonder where the wolf has got off to?"

"Perhaps it has learned to fish for itself," Obbi answered.

"You knew 'twas with us last night?"

Almoor scoffed, "'Tis ours to know and see everything, save when you need privacy. Yet, you should not go as far from us as you have been. We fear for you."

She truly had not realized what she was doing and appreciated the concern she could see in his eyes. Before they got back to the others, she nodded her consent.

*

As near as Donaldina could tell, the MacGreagors did not know precisely where they were going, save for north. She had not often been that deep in the forest either, and for all she knew they were lost. Only the sun could tell them which way was north, and the sun did not always shine in Scotland. Furthermore, in winter the sun came up in the south-east and went down in the south-west. Hopefully, they would be home…wherever that was, before winter was fully upon them. She had not noticed it before, but just now it appeared the leaves in the trees were beginning to turn.

Her husband often looked back to see to her wellbeing…far too often to suit her. She knew not if he expected her to nod or even smile, so she ignored him. Just when she thought she could not stand being on a horse another minute, Wallace softly whistled to stop them. To her surprise, he came to her and opened his arms to help her down. She glared at him. "I am quite capable of dismounting without your help."

"As you have already exhibited. Yet, you are my wife and 'tis an honor to help you."

She pushed his hands away. "Can we not forget I am your wife?"

"I do not see how. There are six witnesses to the marriage."

"A marriage I dinna want and neither did you."

"That aside, we are married in the eyes of man and God."

"We are not married in my eyes," she grumbled. Arguing, she realized, meant she had to stay on the horse, so this time when he opened his arms, she let him pull her down. He held on long enough to let her get her balance, and then abruptly walked away. When she went to pat her horse's nose and said, "Find water," the men laughed. Just a couple of feet away lay a stream and most of the horses were already drinking. Donaldina rolled her eyes, left her horse, and again began to walk the soreness out. She had only gone a few yards up the path, when she abruptly turned around and walked right into her husband's arms.

Wallace smiled down at her. "'Tis not safe for you to walk alone."

"'Tis even less safe to be this close to you." She shed herself of his arms, and started to walk around him. "Cannae Obbi or Nikolas see to my safety?"

He took hold of her arm, made her stop and turn to face him. "Nay, they cannae."

"Why not?"

"Because I am your husband."

"So you keep saying. 'Tis your excuse for everything you do."

"You are a MacGreagor now and you shall learn our ways. A husband is honored to care for his wife, and his wife takes pride in caring for him. Together, they care for the children and the parents when they are old. 'Tis the way to happiness."

What he said seemed sensible enough, although she doubted it would work. "In our clan, the wife makes demands on the husband."

Wallace let go of her arm and folded his. "If a husband is gentle and kind, and if he sees to all her needs as best he can, then she shall have no need to make demands."

Donaldina sighed. "And if she makes demands anyway, as some wives are prone to do?"

"Then she is given less and less, until she learns to be grateful for what she has instead of regretting what she has not."

Donaldina thoughtfully blinked a couple of times, looked away for a time, and then went to join the men. It might work, she thought, but she doubted it. It certainly would not work on her stepmother. Still, what he said was by far the most intelligent she had heard him say so far and it gave her pause. Perhaps he was a bit more complex and unpredictable than she thought. Then again, if he thought kindness would soften her up, he was mistaken. She put what he said in the same place in her mind that she kept his imaginary castle. When he came back, she watched to see if he took a drink from his ale flask. He did not.

Magnus already had fresh water in his flask and offered it to her. The flask was heavy, so he helped her hold it while she drank, waited until she was finished, and whispered, "He is a good lad."

"He agrees with you," she muttered too soft for Wallace to hear. In a normal tone of voice, she asked, "What is your name again?"

"I am Magnus."

"Thank you for the water, Magnus. Will you walk with me? Your laird claims 'tis not safe for me to walk alone."

Magnus looked to Wallace for permission, saw his nod, and then began to walk beside her. "He is your laird too."

"Aye, I suppose he is...now. Are you married?"

"I am. My wife is Aerica and we have two fine sons. I miss them all very much."

"But your laird took you away when he demanded you come with him."

"He dinna demand it, he asked if we wished it. 'Tis but once or twice a year we venture away from home. All lads enjoy..."

She interrupted him, "Being away from his wife from time to time?"

Magnus grinned. "If my wife finds out, she will drown me in the loch."

"You live near a loch."

"Aye, and a river that flows into the sea."

"It sounds very pleasing."

"We are happy there, and you shall be too." Magnus heard Wallace whistle and guessed he had taken her too far away. He stepped in front of her, playfully took hold of her shoulders, and turned her around. "My brother Karr is married to Wallace's sister,

Catrina. Therefore, you have a sister now…one that shall not shun you. Karr is even bigger than I."

She looked up at him and raised an eyebrow. "I find that hard to imagine." It made Magnus laugh, which showed off the dimples in his cheeks. She had not noticed that before, and wondered if the other brothers had dimples she had not noticed. Of course, they had little reason to grin so far.

When she stepped on the side of a rock and started to fall, Magnus instantly grabbed her arm. He looked terrified, and it puzzled her. "Is touching me forbidden?" she asked.

He helped her get her balance again before he let go. "Nay, but…"

"Go on."

"'Tis that if you are hurt, we must go slower, and we hope to return before harvest."

"You mean you wish see your wife sooner rather than later?" Again, he let her see his glorious grin, dimples and all. "You love her?"

"Aye, she is the reason I breathe."

"You dinna breathe before you married?"

"Perhaps you shall understand some day."

Donaldina took her eyes off of Magnus and looked at her husband. "'Tis doubtful."

As soon as they were back with the others, her horse came to her and so did her husband. She sighed and turned to face Wallace. It was a routine she would have to get used to, she supposed, albeit a ridiculous one. He put his hands on her waist, and as soon as she put hers on his forearms, he lifted her up, and stayed until she was well situated. She might have been impressed with his strength, had she not been so determined to be unimpressed by everything he did. This time, she did not even thank him. After all, it was an honor for him… or so he said. The question was – what was she expected to take pride in doing for him in return – fish?

*

Fluffy white clouds began to cross the sky as if in a hurry to be somewhere, and by noon the clouds were gone. Birds continued their chirping and the strong smell of Scots pine filled the air. The bluebells on the forest floor seemed to be stretching their blossoms upward in an effort to catch the sun's rays, and when she looked back, the wolf was keeping itself well hidden, though it needn't bother for everyone knew it was following them.

"Tosd!" Wallace abruptly said in a tone just above a whisper. Instantly, the men halted their horses and drew their swords without making a sound.

Never had Donaldina known a man to demand silence without a good reason, so she leaned forward and spoke softly to her horse to keep it calm. It worked. When she sat up and worriedly looked around to see what alarmed Wallace, she too could hear men's voices and they were not that far away.

Cautiously, Hani dismounted, moved the branch of a tree aside, and stepped into the forest, while the rest of them quietly dismounted. When Hani came back, he immediately went to whisper his report to his laird. "Two lads and one lass. The lass be tied to a tree with a cloth in her mouth to keep her quiet."

"Tied?" a horrified Wallace asked as he motioned for all of them to come closer.

"Aye."

"Weapons?"

"The usual," Hani answered. "They are small lads and no match for the seven of us."

"Eight," Donaldina softly muttered. She didn't think anyone could hear her, but her husband turned to look at her. Afraid to say more, she pointed at the sword, tied around his waist, and then motioned for him to give it to her. Oddly, her husband did not hesitate, untied the strings, and handed both her sword and dagger to her. She hadn't expected it to be that easy, and nodded her appreciation. His eyes held hers for a moment before he turned his attention back to Hani. He was asking her not to run her sword through his back, she supposed. She quickly tied her sheaths around her waist, and then drew her dagger.

"Nay, Father!" she heard one of the strangers shout.

"I know that voice," she whispered to Steinn. "Wait here." Before he could stop her, she slipped into the forest and a moment later, stepped into a small clearing on the other side of the trees. She suspected the MacGreagors were right behind her and she was right, although they moved without making a sound.

The two men in the small clearing had their backs to her. Just as Steinn reported, the woman with unkempt curly hair was bound to a tree and gagged, but her eyes reflected her joy at seeing another woman. The hostage was wearing a full-length fur cloak that kept the ropes from rubbing, but it also kept the girl from freeing her arms, and therefore herself. Donaldina noticed something very odd about the girl – she was wearing new shoes, the kind normally reserved for the wife or daughter of an important man, possibly a laird.

Donaldina put a finger to her lips. When the girl slightly nodded, Donaldina put her hands behind her back and loudly cleared her throat. Both men instantly spun around and started to draw their swords.

"Donaldina?" Odhan, the elder of the two men asked the instant he recognized her. Odhan was dressed in clothing that had long since worn out, and when he smiled, he showed his chipped front tooth. "You have come at last. Have you missed me?" he asked, walking to her.

"Like a thorn in my foot," she answered. His hair was uncombed, his beard untrimmed, and two of the laces meant to hold the front of his shirt together were missing.

Odhan chuckled. "I knew you would come."

Just as he started to put his arms around her, she placed the tip of her dagger firmly against the bottom of his Adam's apple. "I am of bad humor today, and there is nothing that would bring me more pleasure than to cut you from ear to ear."

Odhan immediately withdrew his hands and held them out away from her.

Bawheed rolled his eyes. "She will do it too." Still in his early teens, Bawheed sat down on the ground and started to lace up shoes that had holes in the toes.

Donaldina knew both of them well. Odhan and Bawheed came to the Bisset village when Bawheed got the same terrible fever that ravaged all of Scotland the year before. It was Donaldina who nursed the boy back to health. He was a good boy and she favored him, but she dare not take her eyes off of his father for long. "Bawheed, you are looking well and I believe you are much stronger than the last I saw of you."

"I am," Bawheed said, flexing his not very muscular arm. As soon as she glanced at it and smiled, he went back to lacing his shoe. "Father keeps me fit."

"He is a good father," said she, still not taking her eyes off Odhan.

"And I shall be a good husband." Odhan leaned to his right to look behind her. "Have you come alone?"

"Nay, I have come with seven giants."

Both he and his son looked up and scanned the tops of the trees. Even the girl looked up. Odhan scoffed, "I see no giants."

"Lay a hand on me again and you shall."

He studied the sincere look in her eyes and took a step back. "We go to barter with your father. Has he come with you?"

"Nay, not this time." To keep them calm, she put her dagger away. Just then, she pretended to notice the girl. Alarmed, she stared at Odhan. "What have you done? Have you taken her from her clan?"

Again Odhan scoffed, "Nay, we have not taken her."

"We did take her…sort of," Bawheed countered as he put on his other shoe.

"Why have you taken her… sort of?" Donaldina asked.

"She sold us a horse that went lame," Odhan answered.

Donaldina giggled. "You bought a lame horse?"

"'Twas not lame when I bought it," he argued.

Her smile turned to a frown. "If that be the case, 'tis not her fault."

Bawheed disagreed. "It is her fault, she sold it to us."

Donaldina put her hands on her hips. "You once sold me a goat and it died."

"That goat died?" Bawheed asked. "I favored that goat."

"Perhaps I should tie your father to a tree."

Odhan's brow began to wrinkle. "Donaldina, you…I…" He thoughtfully scratched the back of his head. "We mean to barter her for another horse."

Donaldina rolled her eyes. "Who would take her? Can you not see she is too unkempt to be of much use to anyone? Her hair is the wrong color and so are her eyes."

"Her hair is the same as mine," Bawheed argued.

"Have you gone blind?" Donaldina asked. "Her hair is red and yours is yellow."

Bawheed forgot his shoes and took a hard look at the girl. "I never noticed that before."

In a softer voice Donaldina said, "'Tis because the fever muddled your mind. You shall be better soon."

"Aye," a confused Bawheed muttered. He looked at his father and shrugged.

"You best give the lass to me." Just as Donaldina hoped, Odhan was getting more and more befuddled too. Like his son, logic was often lost on him. "I've got it, I shall buy the girl from you, and then you shall buy a new horse."

"You would do that?" Bawheed excitedly asked.

"For you I would." She paused for a long moment before she said, "Of course, your father may wish to bestow her on me as a wedding present."

Odhan's eyes quickly lit up. "You will marry me?"

"Not today, naturally, but I shall need a lass to tend me when the time comes."

He was elated at first, but then Odham's smile faded. "Have you taken up your father's bend for trickery?"

"Trickery?" Feigning deep sorrow, she bowed her head "I am saddened. You shall refuse to marry me then, for you would never take a wife bent on trickery."

"Nay I would not...I mean, surely I would." Odhan looked at Donaldina, then at his son and at last, at the girl tied to a tree.

"Which is it?" Donaldina asked. "Shall you give me the lass as a wedding present, or shall you tell my father you refuse to marry me?"

"How could I refuse to marry you, I love you, Donaldina."

Her eyes brightened as she widened her smile. "Then you will give me the lass. I cannae say how pleased I am. 'Twill go a long way toward convincing me to marry you." She went to the tree, pulled her dagger back out and began to cut the ropes.

"Wait," Odhan shouted.

In the bushes, Wallace was about to send his men in when Donaldina stopped cutting and turned to look at Odhan. "What is it?" she asked.

"When are we to marry?"

"Someday soon."

"How soon?" he wanted to know.

Finished with his shoes finally, Bawheed stood up. "In a fortnight?"

Donaldina went back to cutting the rope. "I cannae say. Father shall want to have a feast, and preparing a proper wedding feast can take weeks. Besides, you cannae ask a lass to live in the forest. She must have a cottage, the same as other lasses."

Odhan tipped his head to one side and then to the other, before he got an idea. "Would your father not give us a cottage?"

She stopped cutting again and considered that for a moment. "I believe he might. To see me happily married, he would perhaps give us two cottages. One for us and one for Bawheed."

"You would cook for me, though," Bawheed asked. "My father cannae cook."

"I suppose I could," she said as she finally cut through the rope. She walked around the tree twice, removed the rope, and then tossed it into the bushes where the MacGreagors were hiding. Neither Odhan nor Bawheed noticed when the rope began to disappear. Instead, they watched Donaldina untie the girl's gag. Next she extended her arm, let the girl grab hold of it, and then helped her up. Donaldina nodded toward the bushes and as soon as the girl started that direction, she went back to talk to Odhan. "I best be getting home."

"We can take you home," Odhan offered.

The girl had not walked into the bushes but a few feet when she spotted Obbi with his sword drawn. Abruptly, Nikolas clamped a hand over the frightened girl's mouth. "We will not harm you," he whispered. She was so frightened, she was shivering when he slowly removed his hand, motioned for her to keep going and stepped away. Her green eyes captivated him for a moment, and he was surprised when she did not do as he instructed. Instead, she stayed with him. She half hid herself behind his back and then tightly gripped his arm. In response, Nikolas put his sword away, turned around, and took her to the horses.

All at once, the bushes behind Donaldina began to move and six large men stepped out with swords drawn. Instantly, Bawheed took off running and Odhan wasn't very far behind him.

Donaldina smiled, cupped her hands and yelled after them, "Bawheed, tell my father I promised you a horse."

"I shall," came a faint, far away reply.

With all due haste, Donaldina brushed past the men and went to see about the girl. When she reached them, Nikolas already had her sitting down and was asking as to her health. "She seems well enough," he told Donaldina.

It was probably not necessary, but Magnus and Hani took up positions to guard them, in case Odhan and Bawheed dared try taking the girl back.

When she saw Donaldina, the girl haughtily said, "I suppose I should thank you."

Taken aback by her impertinence, Donaldina's reply was slow in coming. "'Tis not necessary."

"No lass should be tied up like a mad dog," said Obbi. He untied his ale flask, pulled out the stopper, and offered the girl a drink.

"What is your name?" Donaldina asked.

The girl took a long swallow of ale before she answered. "I am Ceit."

"Which clan are you?" Wallace asked.

Ceit took another long swallow before she answered. "Clan Mackay."

"Mackay? I know not that clan," said Donaldina. "How many days have they had you?"

"Nine," the girl answered, "but they go in circles. I knew not the way home after the fifth day."

"Aye, they are known to go in circles. Have they harmed you?" Donaldina asked.

"Bawheed saved me from the worst of it. He said he would tell you if Odhan harmed me."

Donaldina smiled. "The laddie has more wits than I thought."

"Will your father truly give them a horse?" Steinn asked.

Donaldina had a sparkle in her eye when she answered, "After he stops laughing. He knows full well I would never agree to marry Odhan. My father deserves the cost of a horse and more, for making me marry against all earthly good reason. Furthermore, he favors Bawheed, and perhaps he shall keep them where they can do no more harm."

"No more harm?" Magnus asked.

"They have no clan," Ceit answered. "They have been banished."

"Odhan killed Bawheed's mother," Donaldina said matter-of-factly.

"Truly?" a shocked Ceit asked.

Donaldina nodded. "You are more fortunate than you know."

Wallace frowned. "'Tis good I dinna know that at the time, or I should never have let you go in alone."

"You let me?" Donaldina rolled her eyes.

Wallace ignored his wife's protest and turned to Ceit. "Can you ride, lass?"

Ceit nodded. "Aye." She handed the flask back to Obbi, stretched out her arm, and let Wallace pull her up.

"She can ride with me," said Nikolas.

"Or me," Obbi countered.

"She rides with me," said Donaldina, hoping to avoid a possible rivalry between brothers. She did not need his permission, but she was glad when Wallace did not object. This time, after Wallace helped Ceit mount and then got his wife settled behind her, Donaldina was grateful and thanked him.

Not long after they got moving again, Ceit thoughtlessly fell asleep and leaned hard against her. Donaldina woke her up twice, but she did not stay awake long, and again let her full weight rest against the woman who rescued her.

As he had before, her husband looked back often, and at last, Donaldina returned his inquiry with a pleading expression. Wallace halted the men, slid down, took Ceit out of his wife's arms, and carried her to Hani. She barely woke up long enough to get settled in Hani's arms before she dozed off again.

When Wallace came back, Donaldina whispered, "I cannae hold her, she is too heavy."

He quietly confided, "I should have taken her from you sooner. Do you wish to stop or shall we..."

"I am better now. I want to go home…wherever that might be."
Her words pleased him and that was certainly not her intention, but
there was something in his eyes that softened her heart a little. She
dismissed the slight flutter it caused in her heart as simply being more
exhausted than she thought. Donaldina had learned a lesson too.
Instead of bemoaning, albeit silently, how tired she was of riding a
horse, Ceit had taught her how much worse it could be. Hani had ten
times her strength, and seemed to have no trouble at all holding the
sleeping girl. Yet, she doubted it was pleasant for him either.

It was then Donaldina realized she actually had her weapons back.
Of course, she could not escape just now and leave Ceit alone with
seven Vikings, no matter how placid they pretended to be. There
would be time for escaping once they got Ceit back to her clan…if
they could find her clan. It was true, Donaldina had never heard of the
MacKays, and she knew well all the clans that came to barter with her
father. There were other spice markets, but those were far, far away
and everyone needed salt. It was almost as odd as the new shoes Ceit
had on.

By the time Wallace decided to let them stop and rest, Ceit was
wide awake. While the men replenished their water flasks in the creek,
she and Donaldina began to walk back down the path, for there was no
other place to go. Of course, both Nikolas and Obbi were happy to
protect them.

Donaldina expected her husband to object. Had he not said it was
his responsibility to keep her safe? Just when she thought she had him

figured out, she realized she didn't. Of course, she had asked if Obbi and Nikolas could walk with her, and perhaps he thought it over and decided to let her have her way. Again he was being pleasant, and again she vowed it would not work on her.

*

While they rested the horses, the men not walking with the women used the time to make sure the pouches were not rubbing sores on the horse's sides. "Never have I seen the likes of Donaldina," said Steinn as he lifted first one, and then another pouch. "'Twas right dead brilliant the way she talked the lads into letting her have Ceit."

Hani agreed. "She very easily tricked them, as though..." for a moment he forgot he was talking about his laird's wife.

"...as though she has done it all her life?" Wallace finished for him.

Hani lowered his gaze. "Aye."

"I suspect she has," Wallace said, "and now we know why the two lads tried to caution us."

Magnus asked, "How shall we know when she is tricking us and when she is not?"

Almoor chuckled as he adjusted the halter on his horse. "How are we to know that about any lass?"

"I forget," Steinn said, "Almoor has yet to find a wife."

Almoor lowered his chin and looked at his older brother through the tops of his eyes. "I do not seek to find a wife. I am content to wait until she finds me."

Steinn grinned at Hani. "He believes in miracles."

"Aye. Meanwhile, his nights are long and cold," Hani said.

"As mine are likely to be, even with a wife," said Wallace. He found a place on his horse where the pouch was beginning to rub and made the necessary adjustment.

*

When the women came back, and after they stood talking for a time, Wallace gave Ceit a command, "You shall ride behind Hani now."

Ceit looked pitifully sad. "I dinna fancy riding in back."

Wallace could not believe his ears and stared at her. "What be your age?"

"In spring, I shall see my fifteenth year," she answered.

"And have you a laird?" Wallace asked.

She heavily sighed. "Everyone has a laird."

"Do you do as he commands?" Wallace realized too late that he had asked the wrong question.

"Not always. He says if I dinna fancy riding behind, then I dinna have to."

Wallace fiercely frowned. "'Twould be wise to do what this laird says, or I shall be tempted to give you back to the lads who lately had you."

Ceit was not intimidated. "You cannae. They are long gone."

"True. Therefore, if you dinna obey, you shall not ride at all." With that, Wallace walked to his wife's horse and waited for her.

Unconvinced, Ceit looked at Donaldina. "Would he truly leave me here?"

"If he does, the rest of us shall as well. Either ride behind Hani, or walk," said Donaldina. She went to her horse and when Wallace lifted her up, she thanked him. He looked as if he wanted to say something, but decided against it and went to mount his horse. By then, the others were mounted and when Wallace gave the signal to set out once more, they followed.

Ceit showed her pathetic expression to each as they passed her by, but it did no good. Her last chance to ride was with Hani, and when he stretched out his arm, she got a running start, grabbed hold and swung herself up behind him. "I dinna fancy riding behind," she moaned.

Hani said nothing, but he did smile when his chuckling brothers and Wallace looked back. His smile was rare and it showed his missing tooth, but this time he did not care. The girl lost and the MacGreagor's new mistress sided with her husband. It was a good sign and he was well pleased.

Donaldina missed Hani's rare smile. Instead, sitting a horse again reminded her of how tender she was. The next time they stopped, she vowed she would fold her cloak and sit on it rather than wear it…providing the sun warmed the earth enough. That wasn't likely in the thickness of the forest and again, she regretted leaving the English gown behind. The thought caused her to loudly sigh, which made her husband look back. Once more, Donaldina found it annoying. Was she not allowed to sigh without drawing his full attention? Did he not know she would say if she was in need? Perhaps she might mention that the next time they stopped. Anything was better than having him constantly and unnecessarily watching her.

*

Less than twenty minutes later, Ceit moaned. "I tire. Can we not rest?" No one answered her. Another half hour passed before she mentioned an urgent need to go.

Wallace doubted it, but he stopped them anyway. He watched as his wife dismounted, went to stand in front of her mare, and patted the horse's nose. "You wait for me?" he heard her say, and then grinned when the horse nodded.

Donaldina grabbed Ceit's hand and took her into the forest.

"Why do your horses smell of cloves?" Ceit asked when they got back to the men.

"'Tis a stupid question," Steinn muttered. Fortunately, he was too far away for Ceit to hear, but Donaldina heard and smiled at him.

"We bathe them in cloves every night," Donaldina said, ignoring the fact that her husband was waiting to help her mount. "Tonight, it shall be your turn to bathe them."

Aghast, Ceit looked as though she might actually cry, which made the men laugh. Ceit's horror then turned to ire and she defiantly put her hands on her hips. "I dinna like being tricked."

"Nor do I," said Donaldina as she walked right past Wallace and said to her horse, "Here I come." She got a running start, grabbed hold of her horse's mane, swung up on its back, and then leaned forward to collect the reins. "Perhaps my husband shall let us ride in front of him for a time."

Wallace considered it while he got back on his horse. He moved his horse to the side, looked back and motioned for Steinn to move up to protect Donaldina from the branches. As soon as that was accomplished, he nodded for his wife to pass him and then gave the signal for them to move on.

Loud enough for all of them to hear, Wallace asked, "Who carries the cloves?"

"I do," said Magnus. "You fear thieves can smell it?"

"Aye," Wallace admitted. "When next we stop, we best see that all the jars are tightly sealed.

*

Hani had never met a woman who moaned and groaned as often as Ceit Mackay. Moreover, she constantly shifted her position behind him to let him know how uncomfortable she was – as though she expected him to do something about it. Because she could not completely wrap her arms around him, she hung on to his cloak instead, pulling it down until the clasp in front threatened to choke him. Twice, he yanked it back up hoping she would get the hint, but she did not. Frustrated, he decided it was way past time to have a little fun with his brothers.

Hani turned his face to the side and softly said, "Nikolas fancies you," he whispered.

Ceit leaning out as far as she dared so she could see the men. "Which one is he?"

"The lad in front," Hani answered.

There were five people on horses in front of her, and it was impossible to see the one in front, particularly since the path was winding back and forth to avoid the larger bushes. "I cannae see him," said Ceit.

"When next we rest, I shall recommend you ride with him."

"He is not married?"

"Nay, and he wants a wife."

"I see," she muttered. "'Tis good then, for I wish to have a husband."

Hani simply nodded.

*

When they stopped for their noon rest, Donaldina spotted two squirrels darting away from the path. She set out to follow them and just as she hoped, she happily discovered a particular shrub. She lifted a leaf, and sure enough, hazelnuts were encased in sheaths with tips that had turned red and yellow. There was nothing she loved more than hazelnuts…well, almost nothing.

She began pulling them off the shrub and when she had as many as she could carry, she went back to the men.

"Nuts?" Obbi asked. "Where? I shall gather more."

"And I shall help," Nikolas answered.

Donaldina handed the nuts to Steinn. "That way," she said pointing behind her. She went to her horse, untied her sack and pulled the rest of her belongings out. They consisted of nothing more than a change of garments anyway. She laid her clothes over the horse's back and grinned as she led three of the men into the forest.

Wallace, Hani and Almoor began the ritual of checking the horse's hooves and the seals on the jars, while Steinn found a flat rock. He looked around for another rock, found one that would do, began to unsheathe the nuts and then break them open. When he looked up, Ceit was there with her hand out.

Steinn licked his lips, but he handed her the meat of the first, second and third nut he cracked. When she still had her hand out, he left two nuts on the flat rock, got up, handed her the other rock, and then walked away. Curious, he glanced back just in time to watch her let the rock fall out of her hand. Wallace was watching too, he noticed, so he pretended not to be bothered by it and struck out to help the others pick.

It wasn't long before Steinn noticed Donaldina was tricking his brothers with a little sleight-of-hand. Obbi reached over to put nuts in the sack, only to watch them fall to the ground.

"You moved the sack," Obbi complained.

"Impossible," said she.

Obbi picked up the nuts, and then took hold of the sack so she could not do it again. "'Twilll take all day to pick them with just the four of us. I shall get the others."

"I shall," said Nikolas. He dumped his handful into the sack and then made his way back through the bushes.

"He fancies her, I think," Obbi whispered.

Donaldina was surprised. "Does he?"

Obbi nodded. "He is not usually this willing to fetch."

"I see." She thought little of it and moved to the next bush.

"Brother," said Steinn. "I fear I may have blundered just now."

"How so?" Obbi asked.

"I told Ceit that Nikolas fancied her. I should not have, for now I fear we shall have her as sister-in-law."

Obbi shook his head. "I cannae wait to tell Karr." Obbi laughed at the scowl on Steinn's face.

A moment later, Nikolas came back with the others.

"Where is Magnus?" Obbi asked.

"Watching the horses," Nikolas answered.

Hani rolled his eyes and mockingly spoke in a high pitched voice, "Ceit dinna favor picking nuts."

Everyone chuckled except Nikolas. "She is tired," he said in Ceit's defense.

"As are we all," Wallace countered as he walked to the side of the bush opposite his wife. He too noticed her sleight-of-hand and found it amusing. When the sack started to get too heavy, she handed it Obbi, and went back to picking. Without her notice, Wallace watched her let a ladybug crawl onto her finger, and then let it crawl off on a leaf she had already looked under.

If Donaldina had looked at him, she would have seen the admiration in his eyes, but she did not look. Instead, she moved to a different bush and hoped he would not follow her. He didn't.

Before long, they had completely stripped all the ripe nuts off of three large bushes. When they gathered again near the horses, each of them began to crack the nuts and add the meat to their small bags of dried fruit.

Ceit, everyone noticed, was not willing to help, and Nikolas didn't seem to mind cracking nuts and letting her eat them.

"He shall be sorry later," Hani whispered to Steinn.

"Ah, to be that young and stupid again," Steinn sighed. "Take note of all that happens, brother, for Karr shall want to know every detail."

When they got ready to move on, Hani carefully folded Donaldina's clothes and put them back in the sack, which was now only half full of nuts. Next, he tied it on the back of his horse, intentionally leaving less room for anyone to ride behind him. He pretended not to notice how Donaldina was watching him, and when she smiled, he only shrugged.

"Where shall I ride?" Ceit whined when she finally noticed.

"Dinna you wish to ride with Nikolas?" Hani asked.

Nikolas tried not to look too pleased. "Aye, she can ride with me." As soon as she came to him, he leaned down and pulled Ceit into his lap.

Wallace got his wife situated, and then turned to Nikolas and cleared his throat. "She rides in back."

"Why?" Ceit wanted to know.

Wallace didn't answer. Instead, he mounted his horse and then just sat there until Nikolas made her slide down, get a running start, and pulled her up behind him.

Hani waited for it...they all did, and at last Ceit said, "I dinna favor riding in back." The man who never smiled grinned from ear to ear.

It wasn't long before Ceit had a headache, and then her back hurt and she begged to stop. The MacGreagors wordlessly kept going.

*

Nikolas was a patient man. Ceit had fetching green eyes that made her more than a little attractive, but that was before she rode with him and kept complaining. Four times she mentioned she was hungry and there seemed no end to her comments about being tired. As it was, she was the only one talking, which made the men in front and the ones in back pay more attention to their surroundings – in case she was drawing the wrong kind of attention.

"Can you not tell us where your village is?" Nikolas asked at length. Behind him, the others smiled.

Ceit answered, "I am not certain where 'tis now. I am lost."

"Is it in the mountains or near the ocean?" Magnus asked.

"We are forth clan from the ocean," she answered.

The branches of the trees were low again, so Wallace moved his horse ahead of his wife's. "Which ocean," he asked.

"The North Sea, from whence the Vikings come."

Donaldina couldn't help but giggle, which made her husband turn around and smile at her. She would rather he not look at her at all, but his smile was nice enough. He might even be of more good humor than she imagined, but probably not. It was just a temporary moment that passed quickly enough.

"Are the lads not out looking for you?" Nikolas persisted.

"At first they did, perhaps, but it has been days and days," Ceit answered. "They have given up by now."

Nikolas was disappointed.

*

The next time they stopped, everyone had grown more than weary of Ceit's complaining. When she asked for more nuts to eat, Wallace said, "Nay, you shall not have them."

"What?" an incredulous Ceit asked.

"You dinna help gather or crack the nuts, so neither can you eat them."

Ceit pitied herself for a few moments, looked from man to man, saw that they would not return her gaze, and sat down on a fallen log. "I require a horse of my own to ride. I shall ride Donaldina's horse and she can ride behind Nikolas."

"She is…" Wallace started before he noticed the disgusted expression on his wife's face.

Donaldina walked to where Ceit was sitting, put her hands on her hips, and glared at the girl. "Dinna make me sorry I saved you. Had I known of your foul disposition, I would gladly have let them take you to my father. He deserves to have you."

"But can I not ride your horse for a little while? I ride very well."

Struck by Ceit's inability to listen to what she just said, Donaldina paused for a moment. "Very well," Donaldina said to everyone's surprise. "When we are ready, you may ride my horse."

Ceit had won and was more than a little pleased with herself.

Wallace took the cork out of his flask, took a drink, and then held it out to his wife a drink. Instead of coming to him, she abruptly spun around as if she heard something. Instantly on guard, he scanned the forest with his eyes but he heard and saw nothing. Donaldina turned back around and shrugged.

"What was it?" he asked, as soon as she reached him and took the flask he offered.

She finished drinking before she answered, "'Twas only the wind calling my name."

He raised an eyebrow and glanced up at the gentle movement of the leaves in the trees. "After she passed, I sometimes heard my mother call me."

"That must be it," Donaldina said. "I dinna know my mother's voice, but the one I heard was that of a lass. Did you not hear it?"

"Nay, not this time. I have always found my mother's voice comforting; as if she assures me all is well. Yet it frightens you."

"'Tis not frightening, 'tis just very odd for it has never happened before." She stared at the ground for a moment. "I do wonder though, who called out to me yesterday. I feel as though I have forgotten something, or that my father urgently needs me."

"Is that what has been troubling you?"

She rolled her eyes, "As if being married when I wish not to be, is not troubling enough?"

"I remind you, 'twas you who agreed to the marriage while I would have been perfectly content, had you denied me. Did I not make that plain?"

It was true and there was nothing Donaldina could say in her defense. "Perhaps we should strike a bargain."

"What sort of bargain?"

"I shall not attempt to make you miserable, if you will do the same for me."

"Agreed," he quickly said.

"If that be the case, can you not stop watching me constantly? 'Tis annoying. If I am in need, I shall gladly tell you."

"Tis up to me to protect you."

"I assure you, I feel very well protected."

"Good. Now that you have given your horse to Ceit, you shall ride with me."

She handed the flask back and leaned a little closer. "You think I have given her my horse, do you?" Donaldina walked away with a smile on her face.

They were ready to move again, and instead of getting on her horse, Donaldina stood by and watched. When a happy Ceit tried to approach, the horse sidestepped away from her. Arwen even jerked her head so Ceit could not grab hold of her mane. Ceit quickly backed away.

Donaldina tried not to enjoy herself too much, walked to the girl, and took her arm to steady her. "Perhaps I might help." She held out her hand and when her horse came to her, Donaldina took hold of the bridle. Ceit tried three times before she finally managed to get on.

Donaldina let go of the halter, walked away and when she did, her horse slowly began to sit down. To the laughter of all the men, Ceit slid off the side of the horse and got out of the way while the mare stood back up.

"I dinna think my horse favors you," said Donaldina. "Perhaps you might find another to ride with."

"You may ride behind me," Steinn offered, "but if you speak one single word, I shall leave you in the forest."

Ceit was not happy, but she had no other offers, so when he held out his arm, she took it and let him hoist her up.

At last, the MacGreagors rode in peace.

*

Odhan and his son, Bawheed, ran until they could run no more, found the road and wearily kept going. Even then, they remained watchful just in case the giants were chasing after them. As soon as they heard someone coming, they darted off the road, waited, and then quietly hitched a ride on the back of a passing wagon. They were almost to the wide glen when the farmer noticed them, and made them get off.

Therefore, it was nearing evening, and few were happy to see them when Odhan and Bawheed walked up to the Bisset village gates. They waited and waited, but the gates did not open until Odhan finally shouted, "I've a message for Laird Bisset from his daughter."

Hesitantly, one of the gates began to open, the guard stepped aside, and let the two men come in.

"Is he at home?" Odhan asked.

"Aye." The guard closed the gate, and then led the way to the castle steps. He cautioned Odhan and Bawheed to wait, went inside and announced them.

"Do they smell any better than the last time they came?" Laird Bisset asked.

"Nay, and I am tempted to toss them both in the pond."

"You have my permission, but first, I must hear this message from my daughter."

The guard nodded, and then went back to open the door. He took a deep breath and held it as the two men walked past.

Hiding at the top of the stairs, Tearlag held her breath too, although for a different reason. She did not think it possible, but she worried that Mairi had managed to tell Donaldina the truth after all.

Odhan wanted to come closer, but when they reached the end of his long table, Laird Bisset held up his hand to stop them. Even so, he could still smell their unpleasantness. His voice boomed across the room. "What message have you from my daughter?"

Odhan grinned from ear to ear. "She has agreed to become my wife."

Laird Bisset's mouth slowly curled into a smile. "Has she now. When is this wedding to take place?"

"She said you would set the date, for there is much to do in preparation," Odhan answered.

"I see." Try as he might, Laird Bisset could not wipe the grin off his face.

"She said you are to give us a cottage," Bawheed added, "and a horse. Our horse went lame."

"And I am to become your son-in-law," Odhan said, his chest swelling with pride.

Laird Bisset finally stopped smiling and scratched the side of his face. "Tell me, what did you give my daughter in return for her pledge to marry you?"

"A girl servant."

"How clever of her. Be gone with you both."

"But…"

"Donaldina has tricked you. She is already married."

"Mar…ried," Odhan stuttered. "But she gave me her pledge."

Laird Bisset could not remember a time when he had been more entertained. "Was my daughter alone?"

"At first we thought she was," Bawheed answered. "But then we saw the giants."

A tall man himself, Laird Bisset roared with laughter and kept laughing until his sides began to hurt.

"I see not what is so amusing," said Oldham.

"Giants?" Bisset roared. At last, he curbed his laughter and sat up a little straighter. "Be gone. I shall not see either of you again!"

Bawheed hung his head. "Donaldina said she would cook for me and I've a great hunger lately."

Laird Bisset had endured the smell long enough, and waved the two away.

There was nothing more to be said, so Odhan and Bawheed wandered back out the door. As soon as they did, four stout men grabbed them, hauled them kicking and yelling across the courtyard, and then out the gates. Two on each side, they took hold of arms and legs, waded into the pond and tossed Odhan and Bawheed in.

Although the water was only knee high, Odhan screamed, "I cannae swim." The guards laughed and walked away. Odhan and Bawheed sat in the pond and could do naught but watch as the Bisset gates closed behind the guards.

CHAPTER 5

On the evening of their second day, the MacGreagors came to a clearing at the edge of the trees, and discovered a sizable glen lay between it and the next stretch of forest. It was a good place to stop for the night, rest and cook a proper meal. The men pulled the heavy burdens off the backs of the horses, removed their halters, and turned them loose in the glen. As if children finally set free, the horses began to run to the far side of the glen, turned in unison and then came back. Again they ran back and forth, but after the third time they settled down to feast on the lush foliage.

"Now what are we to do?" Ceit moaned. "We shall have to spend all morning catching them."

Everyone ignored her.

To Donaldina's surprise, three of the men began to unpack the food her stepmother sent without requiring her help. It was true, she hardly had to lift a finger in her father's castle, but this was different. Her stepmother said a husband would demand all manner of things, including cooking, and would be happy with few of them. Yet, Wallace said not a word. Instead, he chose the best bushes under which to hide the pouches of spices, and then produced a kettle. In all their hours of travel, she never once wondered what was in their sacks.

Donaldina walked to the edge of the forest, folded her arms, watched the horses graze, and wondered precisely when it was that she stopped plotting her escape. If she was going to attempt it, now would be the perfect time. She had her weapons back, her horse would come to her when she held out her hand, and she could mount Arwen and be gone long before the men could catch and mount their horses. Of course, she didn't want to shame her father, she could not leave Ceit alone with them no matter how irritating the girl was, and now it would be dark in less than an hour or two. Yet the real reason was none of those. She liked the MacGreagors and they liked her…even Steinn. Wallace was not as despicable as she expected a husband to be and perhaps, just perhaps…being a MacGreagor was worth tolerating him.

Almost immediately, she regretted that thought.

While Hani and Steinn stood guard, Wallace set the pot on the ground. He helped the other men gather fire wood while Nikolas unpacked the food Donaldina's stepmother sent with them.

Ceit, on the other hand, looked as though she expected to be waited on. She too had her arms folded, but her expression was one of discontent. She turned her nose up at a log she might have sat on because it looked too dirty, took no time at all to admire the beauty of the land, and huffed when she noticed the fire upon which they would cook her meal was not even built yet. What she didn't notice was the look of despair on Nikolas' face, and the disapproval on the faces of the others.

Wallace dumped his load of dry wood near the pot, and then paused to watch his wife for a moment. She stood unmoving with her back to him but she seemed well enough. At length, he went to fetch more wood.

It was Almoor who decided to approach Donaldina. He held his flask out to her and when she smiled and took it, his heart was warmed. "Are you quite certain you have no unmarried sisters? I wish to marry a lass just like you."

Donaldina passed the flask back and giggled. "I only have five unsightly stepsisters. Will any of them do?"

Almoor frowned and chewed his bottom lip for a moment. "How unsightly?"

Donaldina laughed, playfully swatted him on the arm, and then went back to the camp fire. She stood watching for a moment, and decided she did not enjoy being idle while the men did all the work. If her husband could gather firewood, so could she, so she went in search, albeit in a direction opposite her husband.

*

Since the MacGreagors only brought enough clay bowls for the seven of them, two men waited while the women were served. Nikolas enjoyed cooking and was proud of the meal he prepared for them.

Being second to the youngest of seven hungry brothers, the duty normally fell to him anyway. While the dried meat was not as easy to chew as it would have been, had it been soaked all day, the vegetables were cooked to perfection. He had a whole range of spices and herbs to add to the mixture, plus enough salt to make anything taste good.

Nikolas didn't mean to, but he watched as Donaldina put the first bite in her mouth, closed her eyes, and relished the exquisite taste. When she enthusiastically nodded her approval, his eyes sparkled, and a wide grin appeared on his face.

"I dinna favor carrots," Ceit muttered, which made his grin disappear.

"I dinna favor..." Nikolas was about to say, but when he glanced at his older brother, Hani was shaking his head. It was probably better for Hani to handle her anyway, for Nikolas was about to lose his temper. Instead, he went back to stirring the pot.

"Who are you?" Ceit asked at last, glancing at all the others.

"We are MacGreagors," Wallace answered.

Donaldina disagreed. "They are MacGreagors. I am from Clan Bisset."

Ceit nearly choked. "Bisset?"

"Aye," said Donaldina.

"Nay, she is..." Wallace started to say.

"I have begged to see the Bisset dragon," Ceit interrupted, "but no one would take me."

Donaldina wrinkled her brow. "Dragon?"

"Aye, the spice dragon, they call it."

"I have never seen a dragon. Do you mistake us for another clan?" Donaldina asked.

"I dinna think so," Ceit answered. "Do you not sell spices?"

"Aye."

"Well, when our lads go to fetch spice from Laird Bisset, they always have a tale to tell about the dragon."

"What tales are those?" Donaldina asked.

"My favorite is the one about the two babies. One was born with too many toes and the other with not enough. The dragon ate them and their mother as well."

"Nonsense," Donaldina scoffed. "Never have I heard of such a thing. Your lads lie."

"They do not lie," Ceit adamantly argued. "Another time, they forgot to feed it and the dragon ate three whole lads."

"We were there but two days ago and I saw no dragon," said Obbi.

"Nor did I," Wallace agreed.

"Perhaps it has died," said Ceit.

"And perhaps it never was," Donaldina countered. "Did you not say you were from Clan MacKay?"

"Aye."

"Then how is it I know not your clan? I assure you, I know all the clans very well."

Ceit shrugged. "I hear Laird Bisset lives in a castle," she said, expertly changing the subject. "It has fifty rooms, and three hundred servants. I also hear…"

"'Tis not nearly as big as that, but go on," said Donaldina.

"Well, most lasses wish to marry outside the clan so they may escape. Others simply run away. One such lass barely got outside the gates before the dragon was sent to look for her."

"Who sent the dragon to look for her?" Donaldina wanted to know.

Finished with her dinner, Ceit thoughtlessly tossed the uneaten carrots into the bushes and then set the bowl in the dirt on the ground. "Laird Bisset, I suppose." She lowered her voice as if to tell a secret. "I am not supposed to say, but his eldest daughter is dull-witted."

"Which? Laird Bisset's or the dragon's?" Almoor asked.

Ceit giggled. "Laird Bisset's daughter, of course. She is the most unsightly lass in Scotland, and lately he has been trying to marry her off, but no lad will have her." Ceit's giggle soon turned to laughter. She neglected to notice that none of the others were amused.

Donaldina forced a smile, "Now *that*, I can believe."

Seven men, who normally had plenty to say, could think of nothing. Nikolas picked up the bowl Ceit left on the ground, used the water in his flask to wash the dirt off, and filled it so Hani could eat. When Donaldina held her bowl out, he noticed her supper was only half eaten, but suspected she was no longer hungry and he didn't blame her.

Just then, Magnus pointed toward the horses. "The wolf is back and it caught a rabbit." Each of them got up to look, but instead of drawing their bows and arrows, the men watched as the wolf approached Donaldina's horse. The MacGreagor horses were skittish and took off for the other end of the glen, but Donaldina's horse simply watched the wolf come to it. Proud of itself, the wolf dropped its supper on the ground, and then sat down. Arwen sniffed the rabbit, and then nodded as if to give its approval. The wolf picked up the rabbit, and then headed for the people.

Frightened, Ceit squealed and tried to hide behind Steinn.

Steinn was not pleased. "You need not fear. The wolf already has his dinner."

To no one's surprise, the wolf paid no attention to the others, dropped the rabbit in front of his longtime friend, Donaldina, and once more sat down to await approval. Donaldina looked at Obbi and said, "I am caught, I see," She knelt down and rubbed the wolf behind the ears. The wolf picked its kill back up, took it to the edge of the small clearing, lay down, and began tearing the rabbit apart.

"'Tis forbidden to keep a gray wolf," Ceit said as she peeked out from behind Steinn.

"Forbidden by whom?" Wallace asked. "I say 'tis not forbidden. If my wife wishes to keep a wolf, I shall allow it."

She might have been happy that her husband had taken her side. Instead, she muttered, "Allow it?" This time when she looked at him, he was smiling, and she almost returned his smile.

"How long have you had the wolf?" Hani asked. "Almoor fancies animals, particularly dogs. Dinna be surprised if the wolf fancies him back."

"I shall be glad of it, if it does," said Donaldina. "I found it in the forest with an injured hind leg. It was unable to hunt, so I fed him each day until the wound healed. I have never seen the pack, although we have heard them howling from time to time."

"Has the pack come with it, do you imagine?" Ceit asked. "I shall not likely sleep through the night knowing a pack of wolves might eat me."

Nikolas was not the only one who had to bite his tongue. Instead he asked Donaldina, "Your horse befriended the wolf too?"

"'Tis the first I have seen of that myself," Donaldina admitted. "The wolf will likely keep following. Shall it upset your horses?"

Wallace looked at the horses in the glen. They seemed to be content to go back to their grazing. "Besides, 'tis not *my* horses, 'tis *our* horses, wife."

Donaldina rolled her eyes. "So you keep insisting." She once more walked to the edge of the glen, folded her arms and turned her back to the others. She was upset, but she was determined not to let them see. Was that what all the clans thought of her – that she was dull-witted and unsightly? Perhaps so, although her father often remarked on her beauty. Still, his was the only opinion she ever remembered hearing, and he was likely not objective on the subject.

Wallace spread his cloak on the ground where he wanted his wife to sleep, waited for a time and when Donaldina did not come back, he went to her.

She had a tear in her eye when she finally noticed him.

"If you wish," he said, "Nikolas shall teach you how to read the stars. Nikolas dinna know it, but the clan often comes to hear him, for there is no better way to put the children to sleep."

She turned away and wiped the tear off her cheek. "I would like that very much."

"Of course, you might be too dull-witted to know which is the moon and which are the stars."

Donaldina softly giggled. "I shall learn it as best I can."

Neither of them spoke while she composed herself, "I have made a bed for you," he said at length.

"Thank you, I am very tired." She walked back to the others, only to find Ceit sitting on her husband's cloak. She took an exasperated breath, and then decided to ignore that indiscretion. Enough had already been said, so she spread her cloak beside the girl, lay down and wrapped herself up. The sky yielded no moon, and it did not appear Nikolas was in the mood to talk about the heavens anyway. Even so, it wasn't long until she closed her eyes and started to fall asleep.

"You dinna have a wife either?" Ceit asked Obbi.

Donaldina opened one eye and then the other. "Perhaps you might let the lads rest now."

"But I dinna wish to sleep yet."

Donaldina sat up and narrowed her eyes. "Then perhaps you might stand watch. After all, the dragon may well have followed me."

"You said there was no dragon."

"I lied," said Donaldina. She lay back down and again wrapped her cloak tight around her.

Ceit begrudgingly lay down too and just then remembered the wolf. Slowly, she scanned the forest for any detectable movements. She couldn't see much. "I dinna..." she started to say. Just then, the wolf lifted its head near the edge of the forest and softly growled. Ceit pulled Wallace's cloak tighter, and then covered her head with the hood.

*

Normally, Laird Bisset's days were filled with seeing to the needs of the clan, riding out across his land to see how the planting or the harvest was progressing, and selling spices to Scottish clans. That meant he was far too busy to keep up with his wife's endeavors. Lately, Tearlag had taken to going for a walk after the evening meal and especially after he had enjoyed a bit too much ale. When he asked his guards what she was up to, they admitted there were rumors, but would not say what the rumors were about. Therefore, he could but find out for himself.

That night after she left, he followed her. Twice, he had to dart behind a cottage to keep her from seeing him when she glanced back. She turned down one path, and then another until she came to a particular cottage and knocked on the door. Once more, he darted out of sight, waited for the door to open and for his wife to disappear inside. As soon as the coast was clear, he snuck around to the back of the cottage, and took up a position next to an open window.

He recognized Nathair's voice immediately.

"What news have you?" Nathair asked, as he greeted his sister. "Has he agreed to make me his second in command finally?"

She was reluctant to say it. "I have not yet broached the subject."

"Why not? We had an agreement and I have kept my part of the bargain. Now 'tis time for you to keep yours."

"Brother, it will not do to rush him. Once he says nay, his mind is made up and he shall not be moved. I must wait until he is of a particular mood."

"Meanwhile, I must work in the fields. I would do well as second in command, and you have often agreed."

"I do agree," she soothed, "but if he says nay, our plan is lost to us forever. The only way to rule the clan is to get rid of him, and we cannae do that until you are well settled as the next in line for laird. You must be patient, very, very patient."

Laird Bisset had heard enough, left his position and went back to his castle. So enraged was he, that he picked up his goblet of ale and threw it against the wall. Deep in thought, he began to pace the length of his Great Hall. "Five wives," he muttered, "and each is worse than the one before." He stopped and looked at the fine, gold-handled sword on the wall that he had given to Donaldina's mother. "Lanie, how much I miss you still."

*

To Ceit's delight, the wolf was gone by the time Obbi woke her the next morning. She tried her best to postpone their departure, mumbling about this and that, asking for food, and complaining of soreness in her backside. Nothing worked. Her last hope was that the men would spend half the day trying to catch their horses, but when Wallace whistled, all the horses came, even Donaldina's. Ceit was bitterly disappointed.

As she always did, Donaldina rubbed her mare's ears and nose. "Miss me?" Arwen nodded, which brought a smile to all their faces…save Ceit's.

"If only I had a horse of my own to ride," Ceit whined.

"If only you could tell us how to take you home," Obbi shot back. It was his turn to let her ride behind him, and he was not looking forward to it.

Ceit pouted, "You need not be so cross."

Steinn leaned his face into hers. "'Do you not understand? If you find all you see disagreeable, then disagreeable is all you shall ever find."

She decided she did not fancy Steinn either, turned up her nose and went to ride behind Obbi.

*

The unfamiliar woman was as beautiful as she was determined.

She wore a purple gown and a warm cape reserved for the wealthiest in England, and had her light brown hair in a long braid that hung down the middle of her back. From her hiding place in the nearby clump of trees, she watched the tall wooden Bisset gates open. Shortly thereafter, a weeping woman and an infuriated man walked their horses out, followed by four clansmen with swords drawn. Fascinated, she waited until the swordsmen went back inside, closed the gates, and then waited still longer until the man and woman rode away.

When it appeared all was calm once more and with her English guard behind her, she slowly walked her horse toward a place she had heard about since her youth. It was just as her grandfather said it would be. She paused, looked up at the same castle window where her mother last saw her father, and waited for the village guards to open the gate.

When they did, she and her ten member guard, each wearing matching red tunics, walked their horses through the gates. Once inside, but not yet close to the castle, she held up her hand to stop her guard, and then slowly approached the castle alone.

A man of not more than twenty took up a firm position in front of the castle door. Already that morning, he had witnessed his furious laird banish his fifth wife and her brother, and knew what a foul mood he was in. Now, the English were here and rather than have to go inside to announce the strangers, he decided shouting would bring his laird outside instead.

"What business have you with us?" he yelled.

"You need not shout, I am not hard of hearing," said the woman. "I have come to see Laird Bisset. Is he within?"

"Aye," he shouted. "Why does an English lass bring so many English guards with her?"

The castle door abruptly opened and Laird Bisset stormed out. "Good heavens, John, what is…" He stopped cold and stared at the young woman on the horse. It took a moment, but as soon as he gathered his wits, he asked. "Who are you?"

"I have come to tell you that the wife you banished is dead."

"She is…" He looked hard at the face of the young stranger. Amazingly, she looked a lot like, but not exactly like, Donaldina. Yet, this woman was shorter and her hair was darker still. "I am grieved to hear it."

"Are you?" she asked, not bothering to hide her bitterness. "She loved you to the end. I, however, cannae abide the sight of you. I have come to find my sister. Is she within?"

He hardly knew what to say, but somehow managed to mutter, "Married these two days and gone north."

"Where in the north?" she demanded. All the shouting made her horse begin to dance. Even so, not once did she take her eyes off her father.

"I know not," he admitted.

"Of course not. You knew not where I was all these years. What name did you give her?"

Laird Bisset glanced at the Englishmen and then at all the other eyes watching him. He squared his shoulders and answered, "You waste your time, she is long gone."

The woman turned her horse around and started to leave.

"Wait."

With her back to her father, she halted and asked, "What?"

"What is your name?"

She did not bother to answer, and when the gates again opened, she galloped through and turned north. As quickly as they could, her guard raced to catch up.

For a very long moment, Laird Bisset stood on the steps of his castle staring at the open gates. Suddenly, he turned, ran into his castle, and bounded up the stairs. He threw open the window on the second floor and leaned out, hoping to catch another glimpse of her, but she was already out of sight. Laird Bisset hung his head for a time, and then went back downstairs. He left his castle, walked out the gate and went to the graveyard.

The polished black stone he placed in remembrance of his wife all those years ago seemed to be taunting him. Sluggishly, he sunk to his knees in front of the stone. "You were alive... all these years," he moaned. In pure agony, he closed his eyes. "Lanie, my beloved Lanie. Can you not forgive me?"

He lowered his body until he lay prostrate on the ground with both of his arms stretched straight out. "I beg of you, do not let your daughter find mine – not for my sake but for Donaldina's."

*

Every man except Wallace had taken a turn hauling Ceit behind them at least once. Each time, she managed to be irritating, either by what she muttered or how she hung on to their cloaks. Just now, she was behind Hani again, much to his consternation.

It was almost time to stop and rest the horses again when the animal path began to widen. Not long after that, Magnus raised his hand to stop them. In the distance, he could hear the chopping of wood, and soon they all could. Wallace signaled for the MacGreagors to leave the path and find a place in the forest to hide. It meant going back a short distance and then turning into the thicker bushes and trees. As soon as he was satisfied that they were out of sight, he nodded for Magnus to see what lie ahead.

Ceit tried to dismount, but Hani stopped her with his arm. Not only that, Wallace gave her a stern look of disapproval, which she returned with a flippant expression.

It seemed like forever before he came back, and when he did, Magnus whispered, "One lad chopping down a tree."

"No others?" Wallace asked.

"None that I could see, but I smell smoke. We are likely near a village."

Wallace pointed at Nikolas and motioned for him to go east. Next, he pointed at Steinn and sent him west. As soon as they were gone, he leaned closer to Magnus and said, "Go back to the path and see where it leads." He waited for his guard's nod, looked to see that his wife was okay, and then looked at Ceit. Ceit was clearly put out over having to stay on the horse, but he was not persuaded. He did notice Donaldina move her body back to a place where the horse's behind offered more padding.

Magnus was not gone long before he came back to give his report. "'Tis a village and a wide moor to cross before we can enter the forest on the other side. We could go around, but I say we see if they know how to find clan MacKay."

Wallace hardly had time to agree before both Nikolas and Steinn came back. "Are we in danger, lads?"

"Nay," Steinn answered. "I see and hear naught but the lad chopping wood."

"Perhaps we might ask him how to find the MacKays," Wallace said. He turned to stare at Ceit.

"I fancy staying with you," Ceit said. Yet again, she was ignored and this time she noticed. Put out, she looked at the palms of her dirty hands and tried to wipe them on the back of Hani's cloak.

Wallace motioned for them to go back to the path, and began to talk loudly so the woodsman could hear them coming. The path led them back to the same road they had departed from after they left the Bisset village. It ran alongside a wide glen, just as Magnus said. Following the road one direction would take them further north, but the other direction led to a village he could see in the distance. Wallace nodded for them to go to the village.

The beauty of the moor took Donaldina's breath away. Scottish blackface sheep grazed on the side of a hill in the distance. An Irish setter with bright red fur was at work keeping the sheep from wandering off, but the most remarkable sight was of the spotted black and white Jacob sheep with four horns, two that curved toward the animal's mouth, and two that stood straight up. Not often had she seen those. Birds happily flew from one side of the glen to the other, and two rabbits scurried under a bush to get out of sight.

As they turned toward the village, the men watched for the woodsman, but he had gone into hiding just as Wallace hoped. Now that the road was wide enough and while she took in the beauty of the land, Wallace pulled his horse up next to Donaldina's. He too enjoyed the sight, but he paid more attention to how fond she appeared to be of it.

The village had no spiked wooden fence, nor any gates to protect them, but then this village was at least two days away from the English and except for thieves who wished to steal their sheep, they likely had little to fear. Both the old and new cottages had enough land between them for vegetable garden patches, and some had flowers still blooming, although it was quite late in the year. Furthermore, the grounds were kept remarkably clean, despite cows, dogs, and horses that were allowed to wander about.

The clan's Keep, where all the important business took place, was a spread out, one story wooden structure with a guard tower on each end. Before they even got close, some of the people came into the courtyard in front of the Keep to see who they were. Donaldina smiled to let them know they meant no harm and the very large men she was with kept their weapons in their sheaths. None of the MacGreagors noticed Ceit trying to hide her face behind Hani. As soon as they entered the courtyard, the MacGreagors stopped and waited to see if they would be welcomed or turned away.

It wasn't long before a man stepped through the crowd to greet them. He was especially amazed to see them, since he had not passed them on the road after he took Mairi's body home. Somehow he managed to get in front of them. "Donaldina, can it be you?" he asked.

"Conall MacTavish, 'Tis good to see you again," she said, moving her horse forward. "You live much farther away than I suspected."

He shrugged. "Well, you are certainly welcome." He looked beyond her at the strangers. "Who might they be?"

"They are MacGreagors," she answered.

He wrinkled his brow and pretended not to know about her marriage. "Have they taken you?"

"Not precisely," she answered.

The man with a great memory pretended to figure it out. "One has had the good sense to marry you, finally?" His grin widened when she begrudgingly nodded. "Which one?"

"That one," she answered as she tipped her head toward Wallace. "He is Laird MacGreagor."

"A laird? I am well pleased," said Conall. He looked at Wallace and nodded his greeting. "I was convinced she would never consent to marry. Laird MacGreagor, you've no idea what a fine lass she is. Come, Laird MacTavish shall wish to meet you." He stepped away so they could dismount, and was shocked at what he saw behind one of the men. Conall slowly shook his head and closed his eyes. When he opened them again, Ceit was off the horse glaring at him with her hands on her hips.

"Well, now," Conall sighed, "you have come back, I see."

"Brother, I dinna favor these MacGreagors."

"I suspect not," he said. "You best go home. Mother has actually missed all your complaining. I, on the other hand, have not."

The eyes of every MacGreagor watched, and more than one sighed their relief, as Ceit scampered off toward the center of the village.

"She is your sister?" Donaldina asked. "She said she was a MacKay."

"Ceit is not always honest, as I am certain you have learned by now. We've no hope of a husband for her, but Laird MacTavish does his best to find her one." Conall threw out his arm in the direction of the Keep and then followed Donaldina to the steps. "Have you met Laird MacTavish?"

"How odd. I do not recall ever meeting him," Donaldina answered. "Does he not always send you?"

"Always. He is not so good at riding, for he is…well, you shall see for yourself." He held the door for the guests, followed them in, and was not surprised when they stopped just inside the door.

At the other end of the room sat a man of considerable width. They tried not to stare, but he sat in a chair twice the size that was common, and wore a very long tunic loosely tied at the waist with a gold braid. Below the tunic, the bottoms of his long pants covered his shoes up to the toes. Yet, his red hair was neatly tied back, and his mustache and beard were trimmed and combed.

"Come closer," Laird MacTavish said, his voice echoing in the long room. He waited while all eight MacGreagors came to stand in a row before him with Wallace and Donaldina in the middle. Conall quickly went to stand on the right side of his laird facing the MacGreagors. "Laird MacTavish, Laird MacGreagor, and his bride have come to see you. His bride is Laird Bisset's daughter."

"You are Laird Bisset's daughter?" MacTavish asked.

"Aye," said Donaldina.

"Tell me, how does your dragon do?"

When she looked, Conall's cheeks were puffed. She narrowed her eyes and glared at him. "Apparently, I am too dull-witted to know."

At the realization, Laird MacTavish was nearly speechless. "You are Laird Bisset's eldest daughter?"

"So I have always believed," she answered.

"But you are not unsightly at all. Rather, you are quite handsome." He too turned to glare at his messenger. "Conall, I demand an explanation."

"She has so many sisters, I must have been mistaken."

"Mistaken?" Laird MacTavish asked a little louder than was necessary. "I find that hard to believe of a lad who remembers every word ever spoken to him. Come now, what have you done?"

Conall bowed his head. "Ceit plagues me each time I come home, for news of the outside world. When there is little to be had, which is more often than not, I…"

"You tell her lies?" MacTavish interrupted.

Conall swallowed hard. "Stories, just silly stories. Do forgive me. I dinna think Ceit would tell you."

The great and powerful laird of the MacTavish clan was quiet for a time. "Am I to understand there is no dragon?" No one answered, and at length he took his eyes off of his messenger. The room fell so deadly silent, they could hear a rat scurrying across the room and a bird chirping outside.

"Surely, you dinna believe there was," Conall asked.

At first, Laird MacTavish's belly began to jiggle, then his mouth opened wide, and then…loud rounds of laughter burst forth. "I paid Ceit a handsome pair of shoes each time for her stories." A few seconds later, the door to his Keep flew open and three guards came to see what was the matter. Laird MacTavish could not stop laughing, but he managed to wave his guards away. His laughter was so infectious, the guards began to laugh with him. Even Donaldina started to laugh and her husband could not help but smile. The brothers were so happy to be shed of Ceit, they would have thought anything comical.

"Bring food," Laird MacTavish commanded. Immediately, a side door opened and six strong men entered. As soon as the MacGreagors got out of the way, they picked up the long table, carried it to their laird so he would not be put upon to move, and then brought the chairs. In the midst of it all, Conall tried to slip away.

MacTavish was not fooled. "Conall, where might you be off to?"

Conall quickly turned, came back, and found a stool. He pulled it up to the end of the table and sat down.

"I believe we are having dragon stew," MacTavish teased Conall before he turned his attention back to his guests. "Sit down, MacGreagors. You shall join me in a bite to eat and tell me all the news. I hear the Vikings are back."

As was customary when two lairds sat at the same table, everyone else remained quiet and let them talk. "We have heard the same,"

Wallace answered as he took a seat next to his wife. "They raided yet another village near the coast."

"Not your village, I dearly hope."

"Nay, we are two villages away from the North Sea," said Wallace.

"Yet, someday they may well make it farther inland and you might have to fight them."

"And so we shall fight them, and vigorously," Wallace said.

"Where is your village precisely?"

"We have three northern rivers to cross before we are home, but the crossing is easier this time of year."

"True." Laird MacTavish watched as platters of food, goblets and pitchers of ale were set on the table. Unable to resist, he picked up a chicken leg and took a bite. Finding it not quite to his taste, he raised an eyebrow, but decided not to say anything about it in front of his guests. "Is Laird Bisset well," he asked Donaldina.

"Quite well, the last I saw of him," she answered.

"We hear much of the many lads who attempted to marry you. Is it true?"

She slumped a little. Have the clans nothing better to talk about, she wondered. "There have been a few," she answered, "but they were likely tricked by my father."

MacTavish raised both of his eyebrows. "Tricked? I doubt they needed tricking."

She blushed. "You are very kind."

"And there's a first for me," he chuckled. "Yet, I know a fair lass when I see one, and now that I can see you better, I am reminded of your mother."

Donaldina was astounded. "You knew her?"

"Knew her? I loved her dearly. I chose her for my wife, but she preferred your father. It was a mistake on her part, I have always thought, but at the time there was no persuading her."

"Please tell me. What do you remember of her?" Donaldina asked.

"Well, she was…handsome, naturally with light hair and blue eyes that often took my breath away – when I could get her to look at me, that is. Naturally, I was much younger and got out and about more often. After she married your father, I could not bring myself to further visit your village, and stayed away."

"What was her true name?"

Laird MacTavish deeply wrinkled his brow. "You know not your mother's name?"

Just as astounded, Wallace asked, "Truly?"

"Father called her Lanie, but what sort of name is that for a Scot? I asked, but no one else would speak of her except to say she was handsome," Donaldina answered.

Laird MacTavish laid the chicken leg in his bowl, wiped his hands on a cloth, and folded his arms. "'Tis High treason and I blame your father for it. Her Christian name was Elaine. She was English and not Scottish, you know."

"English?" Donaldina gasped.

"Aye. The first I saw of her was at a feast to which the English invited Scottish merchants. She was more than handsome; she was lively and quick-witted. More than a few lads had an eye for her. How I regret losing her. I regret it very much to this day."

Donaldina was thoughtful for a moment. "Tell me, did she wear a purple gown?"

"Aye, she wore it the day I first lay eyes on her. It had gold and white trim. I can see her in it still."

Donaldina bit her lip, looked at her husband, absentmindedly put her hand over his, and was about to cry. "I dinna know 'twas hers. I left it in the woods."

He was moved both by her touch and her pain, but at length he said, "We cannae go back for it."

"I know." When she realized what she had done, she removed her hand and put it in her lap. "We must be home before the harvest."

Laird MacTavish said, "Perhaps Conall can find it for you when next he goes to the village." When he looked at him, Conall nodded.

"Aye, but we shall be long gone by then," said Donaldina. "Do not fret, 'tis not that important."

"Well, I shall have him look just the same," said MacTavish, "and if he finds it, I shall keep it safe for you. Perhaps the MacGreagors shall come back to barter for spices again next year."

"I am quite certain we shall," Wallace said. That seemed to cheer his wife up considerably.

"Where should he look?" Laird MacTavish asked.

"On the path east of the road," she answered. "Thank you, it would mean a great deal to me. I was but four when she died and I dinna remember her, yet I used to pretend she could hear me when I visited her grave."

"I grieved for her myself when I heard she was gone. Only…"

"Only what?" Donaldina asked.

"Pay me no mind," said Laird MacTavish. "I am old and easily confused. I will say this…no kinder lass ever lived than your mother, and I do not doubt she would have loved you with all her heart."

"Thank you, 'tis very nice to hear. My father says the same."

"Perhaps you might eat now," Wallace suggested. "We'll not likely see such a fine meal as this until we are home."

Donaldina nodded and picked up her spoon. She had a lot to think about and her mind raced so, that she hardly knew what she was eating. As the two lairds talked, she disregarded them. She wasn't even paying attention when Wallace asked to barter for a warm cloak for his wife. Laird MacTavish would take no barter and instead had a very fine garment brought in for her, in remembrance of her mother.

*

After a fine meal, and after they were in the courtyard and mounted, Conall came with a bag of food to replace what they had fed Ceit.

"Do the horses smell of cloves?" Wallace asked.

"Not to me," Conall answered. "Follow the road and you shall easily come to a good bridge across the nearest river." It was then he noticed that Donaldina was glaring at him. "What?"

"There were two babies, one with not enough toes, and one with too many. What became of them?" she asked.

Conall rolled his eyes. "'Tis Ceit's favorite story." He paused as if pondering something important, and then grinned. "I hear tell the dragon ate them."

Donaldina laughed. "I shall miss you, Conall MacTavish. Your wit pleases me very much. If you were not already married and if you had asked for me, I would have accepted." She giggled at the exaggerated look of disappointment on his face.

*

Just as Conall suggested, the MacGreagors went back the way they came and then turned up the road leading north. With full bellies and rested horses, they rode two across and remained silent for quite some time.

At length Wallace asked, "Why was no one allowed to tell you about your mother?"

Riding beside him again, she had been wondering the same thing. "I am convinced now that she was murdered, and Father wished me never to know by whom."

"You think your father killed her?"

"I know not what to think...now. I cannae imagine it, but what other answer can there be?"

"Perhaps he was trying to shield you from hearing something unspeakable," said Wallace.

"Something unspeakable she had done?"

"Perhaps."

Donaldina considered that for a time and then asked, "Such as? What could a lass possibly do that would justify her murder?"

Behind her, Obbi suggested, "She might have killed a child."

"Or her husband's brother or sister," said Magnus riding in front of her.

Steinn had a thought too. "Perhaps she tried to leave him. Is he ill-tempered?"

Donaldina paused before she answered. "I have seen him enraged enough to kill a time or two, I suppose. He is stern and when he speaks a thing, we all best obey or suffer the consequences. Is it not the same in other clans?"

"Normally," Wallace answered.

"Of course," Obbi started, "there is witchery, conspiracy, and even adultery to consider. Your mother might have been judged guilty of one of those."

"I suppose 'tis possible," Donaldina admitted. "'Tis also possible I shall never know, lest my husband allows me to come back next year."

Wallace could not help but look at her and grin. "Allows you?"

The men snickered and Donaldina lifted her eyes to the heavens. For a moment, she forgot who he was, and it was more easily done than she expected. It was a pleasant conversation she had with him and she rather enjoyed it, although she was not about to let him know that.

*

When it came time to rest the horses, Wallace took Magnus aside.

"Have I displeased you?" Magnus asked as he followed his laird off the road into the woods.

Wallace scoffed, "Of course not. I wish to ask you a question."

"Very well, what?"

"'Tis about your twin sons. Does one not feel it when the other is hurt?"

"Aye, 'tis quite puzzling. I have grown accustomed to checking them both when one cries out. Why do you ask?"

"I ask because Laird Bisset said Donaldina feels pain when she is not injured."

Magnus stared into his laird eyes for a moment, looked away, and then slowly shook his head. "The dragon dinna eat the twins. She is one and when the other is hurt, she feels the pain."

"Aye, 'tis what I think too."

"Yet, if her mother dinna kill the other twin," Magnus pondered, "what became of it?"

"I know not."

"Do you think to go back?"

Wallace looked up at the trees. "I wish we could. My wife is troubled, but autumn already begins to turn the leaves."

"If she is a twin, do you suppose she has too many or too few toes?" Magnus watched Wallace make his way back through the bushes to the road and shrugged. "I suppose it matters not." He quickly glanced around to make certain they were safe, and then hurried after him.

*

Like all clans, the MacTavish were a diverse group of people, some as honest as the day is long, and some prone to thievery. Not long after the MacGreagors left, six men mounted their horses and rode out of the village. They knew the land well and therefore knew exactly where to lie in wait for them. As fast as they could, they raced up the road, found the shortcut, and then hurried to get ahead of the MacGreagors.

*

This time, Wallace didn't take them off the road for their safety, knowing it led to a bridge over the first river, and they would have to come back to it eventually anyway. Just in case they were being watched, they rode in silence until they stopped again to rest, and even then none of them had much to say. The men did not mind the silence, now that they did not to have to listen to Ceit's complaining.

Donaldina decided she wasn't as sore as she had been the previous day. Instead of immediately going for a walk as she normally did, she was happy just to stand up. Interestingly, she realized something in her regard for her husband had changed too. His constant watchfulness was not nearly as irritating and she could tell he was more relaxed around her. Apparently, one short, reasonable discussion had changed a great deal between them. He was clearly not quite as dimwitted as she first thought...not quite, anyway.

Still mesmerized by what she heard at the MacTavish village, she wanted to say something, but her husband was busy doing all the things the men normally did while they rested. She watched Wallace check the underside of one of the pouches and discover it was still rubbing against his horse's side. To prevent it from causing a sore, he took out his dagger and trimmed the excess leather. Next, he adjusted both the bags, and put his dagger away.

When he turned, he looked surprised to find her standing close by. "Is there something..."

"Nay, I was just watching."

"Are you certain? You need only ask."

"Thank you." She wrinkled her brow. "Now that you mention it, there is one thing."

"What?"

"Well, everyone is being so quiet, I wondered if you prefer we dinna speak."

He smiled. "I dinna think you cared what I prefer."

Exasperated, she huffed and walked to her horse. There was no pleasing that one, she decided. Before she had time to mount, he lifted her from the back, waited until she got her leg over and then let go. Donaldina ignored him and looked at Obbi. "Is he always this unruly?" Obbi nodded. Standing beside him, Nikolas shook his head. It made her smile in spite of her annoyance.

The MacGreagors had ridden for a time more before Wallace caught his wife's eye and said, "If you wish to speak now, I shall allow it." He followed his decree with a smile, and in a little while she slightly smiled back, but she did not speak. "Go on, I am listening."

Donaldina wanted to ignore him, but there was something else weighing heavy on her mind. "Long ago," said she, "I overheard a lass mention twins. I merely wished to see them, but when I asked, Father flew into a rage. Without explanation, he ordered me to my bedchamber." Donaldina looked away for a time, and then continued, "Is it not odd that Conall told his sister a fable about twins born in our village?"

Wallace gave her question some thought. "Perhaps he was mistaken and 'twas in another clan."

She giggled. "Conall is never mistaken. 'Tis true, he remembers every word ever said to him."

"Yet, I can see how Ceit might pester Conall until he made up such a fable. A fable about twins is not so very far-fetched."

"True." As she sometimes did, Donaldina lifted her right foot and laid it atop her horse's back so she could shift her weight to a more comfortable position. "But if not, I happily know I am not one of the twins, for I have neither too many toes nor too few."

Wallace chuckled. "I confess, I feared the worst."

"Which is the worst? Too many or too few?"

"Too many, for I should have to tell the cobbler about it."

"But too few, and I might easily fall," she said.

"A point well taken."

*

Not but an hour later, they happened to meet a farmer driving a cart pulled by a pair of Scottish oxen. Donaldina tried to hide her face by turning away as the MacGreagors moved to the side of the road to let the cart pass, but the farmer recognized her anyway.

He was surprised to see her. "Donaldina, where might you be off to?" As had happened before, his puzzled expression turned to one of understanding. "Ah, your father has tricked a lad into marrying you, at long last."

She bowed her head in defeat. "He is clever beyond his years."

"Well, I wager you shall be happy," said the farmer.

"I dinna see how." The farmer nodded to her, slapped the reins against the back of the oxen and continued on. "Tell my father," she shouted, "I said to sell you a cow of your choosing for half the barter."

"I shall," the delighted farmer yelled back. "I surely shall."

She watched him go and returned to her position next to her husband, but she was fuming. First, the lads were tricked, then Conall said not, and now the farmer said they were. She desperately wanted to believe Conall. She had never known Conall to lie, but he did lie to Ceit and Ceit told Laird MacTavish. That was it then, the clans had enjoyed their gossip at her expense. Yet, if he was not tricked, why did Wallace not say so? Her irritation with her husband was back full force – a pity too, for she was just beginning to think more highly of him. Oh well, tricked or not, she was married to him and her destiny was decided.

After that, the MacGreagors rode in silence and she was glad of it. She tried not to think about anything at all, and instead admired what she could see of Scotland's beauty from the tree lined road. When they came to a small stream, they stopped to let the horses drink, and then continued on. They crossed small streams, stopped to let the horses drink, and then plodded forward again. Birds continued chirping, an owl occasionally hooted, and like before, the bluebells lifted their blossoms to soak in the rays of sunshine. Normally, that was enough to raise Donaldina's spirits, but it wasn't working very well this time.

Behind her, Steinn said something in the language of the Norsemen. She looked back, but his expression did not reveal what he had said.

"Aye," Wallace said aloud. He soon lowered his voice, but did not look at her when he whispered, "He has seen movement in the trees and fears an attack just ahead."

Donaldina showed no reaction. Instead, she secretly checked to be certain she could draw her weapons easily. She had seen her share of fights between men, but she had never actually been in one. How could she be, with such an overprotective father? Inside her calm exterior, her heart was racing and she knew not what to do or say. She was a good fighter, or so her father said, but there was much he said that she now found questionable. Why did he not say her mother was English, or that the gown had been hers? What else did he not tell her, and how much of what he did say was actually true? She shook those questions from her mind and paid attention to what was going on around her.

Wallace looked ahead as far as he could see, saw that they were coming to a bend in the road, and knew that was likely where they would be attacked. He spoke in a normal voice. "Lads, my wife tires. We must rest."

It took all of her courage not to look around in an effort to see who might be watching, if indeed they were being watched. When they stopped, she waited while Wallace leisurely came to help her down, and when he drew her close as if to hug her, she did not resist.

"If they come, let them have the horses," he whispered in her ear.

She was so taken aback by the unexpected way she felt in his arms, she nearly missed what he told her. Of course, letting them have the horses was absurd, and once more she wondered of her husband's intelligence. As soon as he released her, she took a step back. "Thank you for stopping. I am indeed tired."

Obbi said something in the language of his homeland that made all the men laugh. She doubted what he said was funny, but smiled as though she understood too. That's when she remembered she had not checked the coin and suddenly bent down to look. When she did, Obbi feared she had been hit by an arrow and rushed to her. That alarmed them all.

"'Tis nothing but a rock in my shoe," she quickly assured them. She checked her coin and then stood back up. When Wallace uncorked his ale flask and offered it to her, she realized her hands were shaking and the ale was meant to calm her down. Without hesitation, she took several long swallows.

The distraction was enough to allow Hani to slip away, she noticed after she finished drinking. Now what was she supposed to do? She dared not go for a walk, so she moved ahead of her horse and softly talked to it the way she normally did.

A short time later, Hani came back. He went to his horse, and began to retrieve the rope Donaldina had tossed to them when she rescued Ceit. He pretended to drop it, knelt down, and drew six straight lines in the dirt.

She nonchalantly glanced at the marking as she walked past, and hoped that meant there were only six lying in wait. It helped her relax a little. Six thieves could easily be beaten by the seven MacGreagors, and they would not have to give up either the horses or their expensive cargo.

The MacGreagors appeared to pay no attention to their surroundings and instead, in their language, Wallace appeared to be teasing Obbi. In return, Obbi had plenty to say in his defense, but it was not until later that Donaldina understood what they were discussing – Obbi was being told to stay behind and he wanted in on the fight. Wallace went back to speaking Gaelic and said, "Obbi, tell my wife about the sea monster."

"Me?" Obbi asked. He would have complained more, but he stopped when he saw the scowl on Steinn's face. "Very well. 'Tis not easy being the youngest, but I am comforted for I am the strongest."

Both Hani and Steinn scoffed, but he ignored them and offered his hand to Donaldina. "Would you care to sit, Mistress?"

It was the first time any of them had called her that, and it surprised her. Furthermore, she wondered if he was suggesting she sit, or if she should continue to stand, which would make it much easier to draw her weapons.

Obbi soon realized her dilemma and came to the rescue, "Very well, we shall stand, but let us stand over here. He motioned to a place where two trees grew closed together and provided the most protection for them from behind.

She went to him, and then smiled. "A sea monster? Does it look at all like a dragon?"

"Not in the least, although I have yet to see your dragon," he answered. "What does your dragon look like?"

She tried not to notice as first Almoor and then Nikolas quietly walked into the woods. "'Tis the most fearsome creature I have ever seen. It has yellow skin and one very large, pointed horn atop its head." By the time she finished her sentence, Hani and Steinn were gone too. The last was her husband and she was not expecting the twinge of concern she felt as she saw him disappear. She shook off the feeling and returned her attention to Obbi. "What does a sea monster look like?"

"'Twas when we were but two days away from land that we saw it, or rather it saw us. We had heard that sea monsters were prone to lift a longboat completely out of the water and toss the lads in the sea, but I confess I dinna believe it."

"And now you do," she asked, trying not to appear apprehensive, although she could not help glancing around occasionally.

"I have seen it with me own eyes. There were three, and they were the largest fish I have ever seen. Whales, the Scots call them, but we had not seen whales as large as those."

"They are fish?"

"Aye, enormous black and white fish. First, we heard singing in the deep, and then all at once, they jumped out of the water. Their splash sent so much water our direction that our ship nearly overturned."

Donaldina sighed. "Are you quite certain you are not prone to tell fables the same as Conall?"

"Nay, mistress, you may ask the others," an astonished Obbi said. "We all saw it."

"Very well, I believe you. Tell me about this longship of yours."

"Well..."

There would be plenty of time to hear stories about sea monsters and sailing ships later, so she paid little attention. Instead, the men had not yet come back and she was starting to worry. Yet she had not heard a sound. For a fight, it certainly was turning out to be a quiet one. Obbi was still rattling on when Wallace appeared up the road and motioned for them to come.

Relived, Donaldina got a running start, swung up on her horse and then waited for Obbi to mount. As soon as the two of them set out, the rest of the horses followed and when they went around the bend, Obbi stopped and so did she. She gawked at the six men who had been stripped of their weapons, were without shoes, and stood in a tight circle facing inward. The rope encircled them all and was tied behind one of their backs. Donaldina could not help but grin. Steinn and Hani had the weapons and shoes in a pile at the river bank and were throwing them in, while Nikolas was busy freeing the thieves' horses and sending them home.

It was a sight to behold and it would be a long time before she ceased being amused. A fight without blood and none of her MacGreagors were injured. Donaldina was glad. She was also glad when they set out again and came to a stone bridge over the first river. She had heard of such fine bridges built by the Romans when they occupied the land, but she had never seen one. This one was quite remarkable with three archways that allowed the water to flow beneath it. The horse's hooves sounded like music as they walked across the cobblestones. The trees on the other side of the river displayed even more fall colors and the river gave off its pleasant rushing sound. The rains of the day before had probably raised the water level, but she couldn't tell for sure.

"Has anyone seen the wolf," she asked. She got no reply, so she supposed not.

"Perhaps it got tired of following and went back," Almoor suggested.

She turned in her seat and looked back, but the wolf was not there. Once they were across the bridge, the road turned east and ran alongside the river. Although she could not see it, she could hear a waterfall not too far away and longed to take a bath. Even so, she did not mention it. Perhaps when they reached the next river, she might ask. By then, she was certain they would all be happy for a bath.

It was the first of many large and small Roman bridges she would cross and each time she thought about the coin. What her nursemaid told her years before was likely true. The coin was her mother's and now it was all she had of the woman she never knew.

CHAPTER 6

Conall MacTavish had little to do when he was not being sent here and there by his laird with messages or questions. He loved his wife and children, but he learned long ago that staying in the cottage meant he was underfoot, and his wife preferred him gone. Therefore, he often hung around the courtyard or in the glen watching the horses, the flowers grow and the children play.

On this day, the children were arguing, as tired children often do, so he sent the lot of them home to their mothers. It was then he saw it. Up the back path came six barefoot men and he recognized them all. Conall folded his arms and waited until they were close. "You have lost your shoes, I see."

None of the men acknowledged him and walked right past. "And your horses too." Conall called after them. "Could it be the MacGreagors were not willing to give up their spices?" Again, he was ignored, so he loudly asked, "Have you left them unharmed?" They were about to disappear down different cottage paths when one of them looked back and nodded.

"Good," Conall whispered. He looked at the position of the sun and sighed. Soon it would be evening and he too could go home.

*

Each time the MacGreagors met a rider or a farmer headed for the Bisset Village, Donaldina held her breath while Wallace stopped to inquire as to the news. Fortunately, none of those recognized her. If they did, they said nothing. Occasionally, one of the strangers would give the tall, strong, well-armed MacGreagors a hard look, not sure if they could be trusted or not, but Wallace managed to sufficiently ease their apprehension.

The news consisted mostly of second hand versions of a Viking raid, although none of them were quite certain where it had taken place. Just now, there were no fevers ravaging Scotland that anyone knew of, and the MacGreagors were glad to hear that. However, three brown bears had been spotted in a western forest a fortnight ago. Wallace mentioned the quality of the spices to be had at the Bisset village, and advised them not to settle for the first price quoted. That said, each party wished the other well, and continued on in opposite directions.

When the road took them to the crest of a hill and the trees parted enough to allow them to see the far off land, they stopped to rest the horses. Cottages belonging to farmers were situated in small clusters of three or four. Cattle roamed the lands beyond, except where stonewalls or hedgerows kept them out of vegetable and food growing fields. Men set aside their one row at a time, wooden and iron plows, in favor of using livestock to pull carts loaded with goods being harvested and taken to various markets. Younger children played, while wives and older children helped bring in the crops.

"We are late, lads," Wallace muttered as he got them moving again. "The harvest has begun."

*

For their night meal, the MacGreagors once more found a small loch in which to fish. Donaldina watched for the wolf, shrugged when she did not see it and enjoyed the food the men made for her. That night as she lay wrapped up in the cloak her husband secured for her and looked up at the thousands of stars in the night sky. Happy to have the warmth of his cloak back, her husband wrapped up and lay down beside her. She was a bit ill at ease with him so close, but where else was he to sleep?

Lying not far from her, Nikolas said, 'Odin's Wain'."

"What?" she asked.

"'Tis 'Odin's Wain' you are seeing."

"Where?"

He pointed at the first star, traced the handle to the cart, and then outlined the cart.

She was delighted. "Oh, I see it now."

"'Tis without the horses, but 'tis a cart right enough. Odin is the Viking god of nearly everything, good and bad. I found his stories most confusing."

"You are not Catholic?"

"We are now," is all Nikolas was willing to say on the subject. "Over there is a collection of stars. They are not as bright as most, but if you look long enough you shall see lasses dancing." He paused and watched her face until her smile came back. "In spring I shall show you the warrior's belt. 'Tis three stars perfectly aligned. Also in spring…" He kept talking until Wallace nudged him, and when Nikolas looked, Donaldina was sound asleep.

*

In the deep blue just before sunrise, Donaldina awoke to find the men up and busy again. She sighed, sat up, brushed the dirt out of her hair, and then looked longingly at the water. "Have I time to bathe?" She was delighted when Wallace nodded, and headed for the shore. Just in case, she looked back. Assured they were not watching, Donaldina undressed, pulled the string off the end of her braid, unbraided her hair, and walked into the water. The water was cold, but she did not care. It felt glorious to be getting clean again.

With their backs to her, the men busied themselves getting the horses loaded, and then cracked the remainder of the nuts, divided the nut meat among them, and added it to what was left in their small dried fruit sacks. It wasn't much, but they had saved most of the bread given to them by Laird MacTavish.

When she looked a second time, the men had finished their chores, were standing with their backs to her and she knew it was time to get out. She submerged long enough to swish the water through her hair, got out in a hurry, and dressed faster than she ever had in her life.

"Now we bathe," Obbi announced. "Promise you shall not watch?"

Donaldina giggled, turned her back to the water, and began to comb the tangles out of her hair. It would take half the day to dry enough to braid it again, but she couldn't help that.

*

It was mid-morning when Wallace said to his wife, "'Tis a good day."

"Um," she agreed. It was a good day…so far. The sun was warming the air and because the farmers were tending their harvest, they had not yet encountered anyone on the road who might know her.

"The lads got a good night's rest, the horses are healthy, and we shall likely make it home sooner than we thought," said he. "Are you well?"

Surprised by his question, she frowned. "Do I not seem well to you?"

He chuckled. "You seem quite well, but you are not prone to complaining. I fear you will not say when you are in need."

"I need to be off this horse," she grumbled.

"That, I cannae help you with. Nevertheless, we shall stay on the main road now."

"Is it not more dangerous?"

"Perhaps, but we hear of no clan wars and 'tis impossible to avoid all danger." When they came to a fork in the road and stopped, Wallace asked, "Which one, lads?" Three of them said left and three said right, prompting Wallace to look to his wife to break the tie.

"Which is the way to the North Sea," she asked. As soon as her husband pointed right, she said, "I say we go left. I dinna wish to see what the Vikings have done."

"Agreed," he said and nodded for Magnus to take them left.

Two hours later, the road led down a hill and across a wide glen where farmers were hard at work. Before they came to a collection of cottages, Wallace stopped them and got down. To the farmer in the field, he nodded and when the farmer headed toward him, Wallace walked out to meet him.

"We seek to barter for food, if you have it to spare," said Wallace.

There was a measure of mistrust in the farmer's eyes. "'Tis she your wife?"

"Aye."

"And if I ask, will she say the same?"

Wallace threw out his hand to indicate the farmer was free to do as he wished. He ignored the farmer's sideways glare and followed him to Donaldina.

As she had become accustomed to doing, Donaldina kept her face turned away lest she be reminded of her father's trickery. "Lass?" she heard an unfamiliar voice ask. There was nothing she could do but turn to look at him. "Luke? Is it truly you?"

The farmer's face instantly lit up. "Donaldina? Fancy meeting you here." He forgot what he intended to ask for a moment, and then remembered. "The lad says you are his wife."

"Aye, he tells you true," she answered.

As though no one else was there, his smile returned. "I meant to come for you myself, but I am too late, I see. Is he a good lad?"

She glanced at Wallace before she answered, "He is a bit tiresome, but I hear most lads are when first they marry."

"Tiresome?" Obbi whispered too quietly for anyone else to hear.

"Luke, I dinna get a chance to say how sorry I was for the loss of your wife." Finally remembering the MacGreagors, she explained, "She was thrown from the horse Luke bartered from my father. They were not yet out of my father's courtyard when it happened."

"'Twas no one's fault," Luke assured her, hurrying to change the subject. "Your husband wishes to barter for food, shall I let him?"

Donaldina rubbed her belly. "My stomach says aye." She returned his grin and let her husband help her dismount. "So this is the land you often boasted of. 'Tis fine land indeed," she said as she started to walk down the road between her husband and her old friend.

Luke turned back to look at Magnus. "You shall find water for your horses on the back side of the cottage."

"Thank you," said Magnus. He waited until the three on foot turned toward the cottage courtyard and then led the others to the water.

"You come at just the right time. The crops are good this year and we have more than enough to share. Can you stay for a meal? I cook…"

"I fear we cannae," said Donaldina. "My husband's clan shall start their harvest soon, and we must get home…wherever that is." She smiled briefly at Wallace. "He was tricked into marrying me," she boldly admitted.

Luke frowned. "I would not have needed trickery, and I find myself quite jealous that he has you and I do not. However, if you say he is a good lad, I shall try not to mourn the loss of you – for more than an hour after you are gone."

Donaldina giggled. "I have missed your good humor, Luke. There was so little laughter to be had in my father's castle."

"True. Now, if your husband will gather his food pouches, I shall fill them with enough for…" he abruptly turned to Wallace. "How much longer must you travel?"

"Two days, perhaps three if there is trouble."

Luke nodded, and then waited while Wallace and Obbi collected the pouches. In less than an hour, their food supply was replenished, each of them had eaten a crisp, ripe apple and the MacGreagors were ready to move on.

"Thank you," said Donaldina. "When next you see my father, say…"

"I cannae bear to go back," said Luke. "Cormag fetches what I need these days."

"I understand." She smiled one last smile, and then the MacGreagors moved on. A tear welled up in her eye when she realized she might never see any of the people she knew again, especially her father. Try as she might, she could not hate him no matter what he had done, and so far all she could truly attest to him was marrying her off. No matter what, she loved him and missed him terribly.

"My father gave Luke's barter back and had the horse put down," she finally gathered her emotions enough to tell her husband.

"I would have done the same," Wallace admitted.

She turned to look back. "I wonder where the wolf has got off to."

*

It was not the first time English soldiers had come to the MacTavish village, but to come with a woman was a first indeed. Conall was about to set out to find Donaldina's gown when they rode into the courtyard and stopped.

"Milady?" He asked as she slid down off her horse. "I come seeking my sister. Is your laird within?"

"Aye, I shall take you to him." English soldiers drew the attention of several of the villagers, none of which spoke the language of the southern people, but they could stare at them easily enough.

When the door of the Keep opened and a woman wearing an English gown marched straight for him, Laird MacTavish's mouth dropped. "Donaldina?"

"What?" the woman asked. The table had been moved back in place which enabled her to stand just a few feet away from him.

He raised his hand and shielded his eyes from the bright sunlight streaming through the doorway, "Forgive me, I thought…"

"I am Juliana, daughter of Elaine and Donald Bisset. I have come seeking a twin sister lost to me these many years. Laird Bisset said she…"

Laird MacTavish gasped. "A twin sister?" He studied the woman's face for a moment more. "Yes, I can indeed see the resemblance."

Intrigued, Conall walked around her and went to stand beside his laird's chair facing her. "Fancy that, they are twins."

"What is her name?" Juliana asked.

"Donaldina," Conall answered as he folded his arms. "You have only just missed her."

"Then I travel in the right direction?" Juliana asked.

"Aye," Laird MacTavish answered. "She has gone north."

"Where in the north?" she asked.

"I know not precisely," Laird MacTavish answered. "Her husband said they must cross three rivers before they are home, but…"

Conall could not help but interrupt, "Donaldina does not know about you."

Juliana sighed. "Then that is why she does not seek to find me."

Laird MacTavish abruptly shouted, "Bring ale for our guest." The kitchen door immediately opened. A man entered carrying a pitcher and an eloquent, long stemmed chalice. MacTavish glared at his servant. "You watch me, do you not?"

The servant smiled, nodded, and set the chalice down. "Through a hole in the door."

"I thought so," MacTavish grumbled as he watched the man pour ale in the chalice and then hand it to Juliana. "Have you a report?" he asked.

"Aye," the servant answered. "She brought an English guard that hungers and horses that need tending."

"See to it, then," Laird MacTavish ordered.

Delighted, the servant left the pitcher on the table and scurried out the main door.

"They love me," MacTavish explained. "At least 'tis what they claim. Conall, bring a chair for our guest."

"I thank you, but to stand is more refreshing just now," Juliana said. "How could Donaldina not know about me?"

Conall fetched a chair for her anyway. "Oh there were rumblings, but I dinna know the whole story until lately myself," said Conall. "Even then I could not be sure 'twas true."

"What story?" she asked. She looked at Laird MacTavish, but he didn't seem to have the answer, so she turned back to Conall.

Conall started to explain, "After Donaldina's husband took her away, a lass tried to catch up and tell her, but the lass was murdered before she could."

"What's this?" asked MacTavish.

"I meant to tell you," Conall swore. "Twas Mairi, the one with the scar on her face."

MacTavish did not truly remember her, but he pretended he did. "Ah, poor wee Mairi."

"She was wee no more when I found her," Conall explained. "She had been shot in the back and lay dying in the road. Yet, before she passed, she said Laird Bisset sent Elaine away because one twin had dark hair and not light like his."

"Aye, tis why he sent her away," said Juliana. "He claimed 'twas because she bedded another."

"All these years, I thought Elaine dead. Donaldina believes she was four years when her mother passed, but I heard it was right after Donaldina's birth. Do you mean to tell me your mother is yet alive?" MacTavish asked.

"Nay." Juliana decided to sit in the chair facing the MacTavish laird after all, "He sent her away too soon and she perished in my grandfather's arms. It was Grandfather who brought me up, and just last week decided I was old enough to find my sister. Now, I fear I am too late."

"He sent her away too soon?" Conall asked. "How soon?"

"Less than an hour after we were born."

Outraged, Laird MacTavish pounded his fist on the wide arm of his chair and raised his voice. "Less than an hour? He has surely killed her. 'Tis forbidden for a lass to leave her bed until her issue of blood stopped."

"Aye, 'tis the same in England. She would have suffered less if he had shot her," Juliana said.

Laird MacTavish traded his rage for regret and bowed his head. "If only she had come to me. I would gladly have taken both of you in."

"Who taught you our language?" Conall asked, hoping to change the subject and calm his laird.

"Grandfather. He often has business with the clans, or did before he grew too old. I fear he too shall pass before my sister can know him. Is there nothing more you can tell me about where they have gone?"

Conall answered, "Laird MacGreagor said their village was second from the North Sea. Forgive me, but do you mean to keep your English guard? The English are not well trusted in the north."

"What have you in mind," Laird MacTavish asked.

"With your permission, I should like to go with her and perhaps you might spare a few lads to keep her safe?"

"You wish to go?" MacTavish asked.

"I do. We should know more about the land to the north, and 'tis for Elaine."

Laird MacTavish gave that some thought. "Aye, 'tis for Elaine, rest her soul."

"I recall what I have heard of the north," Conall persisted, "and if any can find them, 'tis me."

"Do you know the rivers well enough?" MacTavish asked.

"Two of them, at least. The third should not be that hard to find."

"Very well, choose four strong lads to go with you, and remember, there are thieves in the woods." He turned to Juliana. "Do you intend to keep going? You are welcome to stay the night."

"I have lost too much time as it is. When were they here?"

"At noon yesterday. They hoped to get home before harvest," MacTavish answered.

"Then I am but a day and a half behind," she muttered.

Laird MacTavish nodded at Conall. "Find her some proper clothing and a fresh horse."

Juliana was surprised. "You will trade my horse for a fresh one?"

Laird MacTavish stroked his beard. "Shall an English horse abide living with the scots?"

Juliana smiled. "As well as Scottish horses abide living with the English."

"The ones we trade for goods?" he asked.

"Aye, and the ones we steal."

Laird MacTavish roared with laughter.

*

With four MacTavish warriors, Conall led the way around the moor and then up the road going north, just as the MacGreagors had. Juliana was an excellent rider and with a fresh horse, there was no slowing her down. If he let her, she would race them onward until the horses dropped from exhaustion. He was determined not to let her, and twice reminded her of the possibility before she settled for an easy gait. When he suggested they stop for the night, she reluctantly agreed and followed him off the road to a suitable clearing.

As soon as they finished the meal MacTavish sent with them, they made their beds, determined the order in which the men would stand guard and sat down to rest.

"Tell me about my sister," Juliana said. Above the trees, she took a moment to admire the brilliant orange and yellow sunset.

Conall did not often get the opportunity to tell everything he knew, which was a great deal, so he began with the day he first saw Donaldina. From there, he told about how she learned bartering and trickery from her father, although he held back the worst of Laird Bisset's swindles.

"Thank you," she said when he was finished.

"Do you wish to hear about your father?"

"I doubt you could tell me anything I dinna already know."

"You know him?"

"Aye. 'Tis he who does not know me."

"How so?"

"He came to our village to barter at least twice a year. I was perhaps eleven when grandfather pointed him out to me. The first few times I watched him from afar, and when I was older and got brave enough, I pretended to spill water on him."

Conall caught his breath. "I have seen him enraged. Did he strike you?"

"He thought to, but his wife prevented him. Even so, he looked me square in the eye and knew not who I was. I suppose it was then I learned to hate him."

"Sleep now," Conall suggested. "We shall leave as the sun rises."

She nodded, found her bed, and lay down. Somehow, she trusted Conall to keep her safe, although they had only just met. He seemed fond of her sister, and that was enough to convince Juliana he would let no harm come to her…if he could help it.

*

When Juliana and the MacTavish guards awoke, a thick fog had rolled in. They ate, loaded their horses back up, mounted, and continued on. In the chill of the moist air, Juliana was more than glad she had a warm cloak to wear. At times the fog was so dense, they did not see a stranger coming until the last moment. Each time, Conall inquired about the MacGreagors, and so far they believed they were on the right trail.

Unfortunately, none of them noticed a split in the road and instead of going inland as the MacGreagors had, they rode toward the ocean.

*

What they saw when the MacGreagors approached the second river, made them stop, dismount and walk to the edge of the water. Like the first, the Romans had built a very fine bridge, but something was greatly amiss with this one.

"I dinna recall this bridge when we rode south," Magnus muttered.

"Nor do I," Wallace agreed. "We have gone farther inland than we intended." Slowly, he scanned the damage. While the bridge looked secure on both ends, it appeared the heavy rains had washed away part of the center pilings, causing the roadway to tilt slightly. He took a deep breath and then slowly let it out. "We must either go east to find a better bridge, or cross the river here."

"We cannae let the spices get wet," Obbi said.

"True," said Hani, "but how do we prevent it?"

"We could build a barge," Nikolas suggested.

"And lose half a day at least building it?" Wallace asked.

"Perhaps 'tis not that deep," Hani suggested. He pulled the
pouches off his horse, set them on the ground, and then mounted
again. Slowly, he guided his horse into the water, and as it began to
walk on the river bed, he watched as the water came up to his ankle,
his calf, and then his knee. Suddenly, the horse found no more footing
and began to swim. The water enveloped Hani's chest and then it was
all he could do to keep his head high enough. Defeated, he turned his
horse around and came back.

"'Tis too deep for Donaldina," Obbi muttered.

"Aye," Wallace agreed.

"Can we not try to cross the bridge?" Donaldina asked. "We could
go on foot with the spices and let the horses swim."

Wallace looked up at the bridge a second time. "I fear risking it."

Nikolas nodded. "I agree. We must follow the river toward the sea
and cross when we can."

"But first we rest?" Donaldina asked. She was more than pleased
when her husband nodded. There was something very calming about
the sound of a river, a light breeze rustled the leaves in the trees, and
she watched as the men emptied their flasks and then filled them with
fresh water. She accepted a cool drink from Obbi, and then thanked
him. With plenty of room to walk down the side of the river, she set
out and soon, Wallace joined her. In no time at all, Magnus and Obbi
got in front of them, and Hani walked behind, leaving the others to
tend the horses.

"Do you still imagine we shall be home soon," she asked her husband.

"I hope so. Perhaps we might find an easier crossing soon."

"That would be nice."

"Do others live in your cottage?"

"My castle, you mean? Nay, my brothers and sisters are all grown and moved out. There shall only be the two of us. My father thought to remarry, but the lass he favored decided against it. If he had…"

Donaldina was not listening. Just when she thought him rational, he dared imagine himself living in a castle again. How did he hope to explain it when faced with the truth, she wondered. How, she also wondered, do you cure a husband of useless fantasies? It was hopeless and a happy marriage was out of the question. The most she could hope for was more time alone – than with him.

*

They were about to start down the river bank to find a better place to cross when Magnus stopped them. "Listen," he whispered.

Each perked up their ears, but it was not until Nikolas pointed that they agreed the ringing of a cowbell was coming from the other side of the river. "Tis going to cross the bridge," he gasped.

The cow mooed, the sound of the bell drew closer, and soon the head of a cow appeared and started to cross the bridge. To their amazement, a second cow, the one with the bell, appeared and then a third. With all three heavy cows on the bridge, the MacGreagors held their breaths and could do nothing more than watch.

"It will not hold," Steinn said just as a forth and a fifth cow appeared followed by a farmer on foot.

With a switch in his hand, and seemingly without a care in the world, the farmer kept the cows moving. Wallace was about to shout a warning when the farmer spotted them and waved. Remarkably, the bridge held, as the first cow and then the others reached the middle and kept coming. Once they were across, the farmer kept the cows moving, and as he passed, he said, "Been like that for months. 'Tis safe, lads, but I'd take it one at a time just in case."

Still awestruck, she watched until the farmer was out of sight, looked back at the bridge and said, "I believe I prefer to walk across."

"So do I," Obbi agreed.

Wallace turned his horse up the road and started across.

"Wait?" shouted Almoor. "I am less heavy. Let me go first."

"Less heavy, but not by much," Nikolas scoffed.

Even so, when Wallace nodded, Almoor stayed mounted and slowly walked his stallion across the bridge. When he got to the other side, he shouted, "'Tis stout enough, lads."

One at a time, three of the men crossed, and then Donaldina walked across with her horse following. On the other side, she walked past her husband and kept right on going. "I find it very pleasing to walk for a change."

Almoor and Nikolas hurried to get ahead of her, and then they too dismounted and began to lead their horses down the forest lined road. "I agree," Almoor shouted back.

Wallace rolled his eyes. They were going to walk for a while, he supposed.

CHAPTER 7

Conall and Juliana were concerned. Not one of the travelers they met on the road had seen seven men and a woman traveling north.

"They took a turn somewhere," Juliana said.

"Aye, but we saw no other road to take," Conall argued.

"Yet, someone should have seen them. Why have they not?"

Deep in discussion, they were not paying close attention, and were about to ride around a bend in the road when a gray wolf scurried out of the forest and sat down just a few yards in front of them. As soon as the wolf began to growl, the horses became skittish and nearly impossible to control. Conall reached over and grabbed hold of Juliana's halter with his other hand.

"What is the matter with it?" Juliana asked.

"I have yet to see a wolf do that," Conall answered as he looked around for the pack. By the time he looked back, the wolf was gone. It took a moment more to quiet the horses and when they did, he took a deep relieved breath.

It was then that one of the men pulled his horse up closer. "Do you not hear screams?"

Conall carefully listened. "Aye, and the sounds of a sword fight. Wait here." He hopped off his horse, and with two of the four men following, he turned toward the sounds and made his way into the forest.

Behind him, the other two men took all the horses and Juliana off on the other side of the road, and found a place to hide behind several tall bushes.

"I smell the ocean," one whispered as he began to tie the horses to tree branches.

"Aye, and I saw a seabird earlier," whispered the other.

"Vikings?" Juliana muttered. When she looked, the eyes of the men were as big as hers.

Conall walked up an incline until he was near the top and then knelt down. Not close enough to see over it, he crouched down and continued. At last, he could see the roofs of a village, lay down on his stomach and crawled the rest of the way.

What he saw horrified him.

The small village faced the ocean and two of the cottages were on fire.

Two longships capable of hauling seventy men each had been rammed up on the beach, and one of them was on fire. With buckets of water, four Vikings worked to put the fire out, while the rest ravaged the village. Scottish men tried to fight while, women and children hid or fled in every direction; Swords clashed, men yelled and women screamed as Vikings dragged them behind cottages.

"We must help them," Conall whispered to the men with him.

"They are too many," one said.

"Aye, way too many," said the other. "We are sent to protect Juliana."

Conall relented. He watched a particular Scotsman ram a sword through the belly of a Viking and wanted to cheer, but he silently shook his fist in the air instead. Sadly, the fire in the longship was put out and the boat did not appear to be sinking. By then, it did not seem that there were very many Scots left to fight. At last, the Viking's carried all they could, including three young women, back to their ships, boarded and rowed away. It was over.

Even then, Conall did not get up. He turned his attention back to the village and watched as stunned people began to come out of the cottages. Bodies lay everywhere, women sorrowfully called out the names of husbands and children, while those that could, fetched buckets and began to put out the cottage fires before the whole village burned down. Three other men checked the wounds, and then began to gather their injured clansmen and take them inside.

It was too much.

Conall turned over and began to slide back down the hill. When he got back to Juliana and the others, he recounted what he had seen. "We must go back the way we came and then ride inland."

"We must help them," Juliana insisted, getting back on her horse.

"Suppose the Vikings come back?" one of the men argued.

"I am going to help. You can come with me or stay, just as you wish." With that, she headed back to the road. The men followed and as soon as they rounded the next bend, the village came into view. Without hesitation, Juliana rode into the courtyard, and dismounted.

"I know how to sew wounds," she said to a gawking woman.

The woman composed herself, nodded and pointed toward the clan's Keep.

*

Juliana and her escort labored long into the night, putting out the fires, helping the wounded and washing the bodies of the dead. At last, it was time to rest and they gathered outside in the middle of a courtyard where someone had graciously made a meal for them.

"'Tis our third time," said one of the villagers as he filled a bowl with salmon filet and turnips for Juliana.

"Why do you not live inland?" Conall asked.

"We are fishermen. We know no other way."

"You sell your catch to the English," Juliana asked.

"Aye."

Juliana took a moment to breathe air free of the smell of blood and then ate her supper.

"The villagers have offered you a cottage with a bed to sleep in," said Conall at length. "We lads shall stay out here and keep watch."

"Then I shall stay too. No need to run them out of their beds, they are far more in need of rest than we." She set her bowl aside when a little girl came to her. She opened her arms and let the child curl up in her lap.

"You are as kind as you are handsome," said Conall. "You remind me very much of your sister."

"The sister we may never find?" said she. "I asked, and the MacGreagors dinna pass through their village either."

"We shall find her," said Conall. "She is but two villages away from the ocean. We shall find her, of that I am certain."

Juliana, took two more bites, gave the bowl back to the waiting woman, and brushed the little girl's unruly hair off the child's face. "Aye, we shall find her...somehow."

Conall nodded to the man seated with them. "This is Ailsa of Clan Wardlaw. They have not heard of the MacGreagors, but he says there is a path behind the village that will take us to an inland road. We shall take it north."

"Good. I dinna care to see more Viking bloodshed."

"The clans fight among themselves too sometimes," said Ailsa, "but few fight with us."

"Have you a friendly gray wolf?" Juliana asked. When he shook his head, she continued. "I ask because one sat in the middle of the road and prevented us from coming sooner. Had it not, we would have ridden directly into the fight."

Ailsa chuckled. "A gray wolf did that? I confess I have never heard of such a thing. Perhaps, if 'tis still around, we might could spare a bite or two." He got up, went to a basket and pulled out two small salmon. He walked to the edge of the forest and tossed the fish into the bushes.

*

The MacGreagors stayed on the main road, and although the men were never complacent where danger was concerned, each of them knew home was not that far away. They crossed glens and shallow water creeks that ran across the road, moved aside when farmers came. As they did each year, the farmers took part of their harvest to a nearby Catholic abbey to pay their yearly tithes.

Each time one passed, Wallace frowned.

"What is it?" Donaldina asked finally.

"I fear we have missed the harvest."

She pulled her cloak apart a little, to cool herself in the warm sun. "I do not pretend to be sorry, for never have I been so exhausted."

"A pity," he said. "For days I have been considering what I would have you do once we are home."

"Am I not to fish?" she teased.

"Not constantly," he teased back. "There are the sheep to sheer in summer, cows to milk and chickens to feed all year round."

"I am overjoyed," she sneered. "Shall I tell you now, I know not how to milk a cow, or shall I simply have a go at it and let the people laugh at me?"

"I shall teach you," Obbi offered.

Nikolas laughed out loud. "You would do better to let a lass teach you. Obbi had eight thumbs and last time he tried milking, the cow nearly kicked him."

"Never have I seen Obbi move more quickly," Almoor chuckled.

As soon as they came to the next glen, Wallace pointed at a hill in the distance. "Look there. 'Tis the land of the Limonds, my father's mother."

"The one hauled off by a Viking?" she asked.

Wallace frowned. "Shall you never forget about that?"

"'Tis not likely." She grinned and then looked long at the blue hill. "We are close, are we not?"

"Aye."

"Yet, I am hardly presentable," she complained.

"Nor is he," said Steinn. He chuckled when Wallace turned around and glared at him.

Magnus said, "They shall be so happy to see us, they shall care not what we look like."

"So happy to see the spices, you mean," Wallace shot back.

"There is that," said Hani.

"If my wife dinna shoot me on sight," Steinn sighed.

Hani frowned at his brother. "Now what have you done?"

Steinn pretended to be bored and yawned. "I prefer not to say."

"Very well, but I shall hear about it anyway," said Hani. "Our wives tell each other everything, dinna forget."

 The bridge over the last river was even more magnificent than the one before and Donaldina marveled at its structure as the surefooted horses plodded across. "The Romans certainly knew how to build fine bridges."

"The Romans," Wallace corrected, "dinna build this one. Scottish slaves did."

"Scottish slaves?"

"Aye. Someday I shall tell you all about it,"

"I am not certain 'tis a story I wish to hear."

On the other side of the bridge, the road took them up the hill she had admired in the distance, and then offered a view of the magnificent land beyond. The beauty was astounding and there was indeed a loch, with a village on the other side that was situated in front of a second hill. "Is that it?" Donaldina asked. She was neither disappointed nor surprised when her husband nodded. There was an odd wall built on one side of the loch, but just as she suspected there was no castle. She tried not to look at him as Wallace waved to men working in their fields, and nodded to women walking on the increasingly busy road. Yet, she could not help but wonder just who she had married.

Just then, the MacGreagors turned off the main road onto a smaller one that curved behind a clump of trees. When they came out from behind them, she heard shouts on the other side of the loch. In an instant, all six brothers got off their horses and ran toward the water.

Wallace laughed and watched as his men waded in and then began to swim toward home. Their rider-less horses knew they were home too, and headed around the loch toward the village.

"Shall we swim or shall we take the long way around?"

Donaldina did not answer. Her eyes were glued to the people pouring out of their cottages, and gathering in front of a high cliff. She thought it was a high cliff – but then her eyes adjusted, and what appeared to be dark rocks in the cliff became windows in some sort of…three-story castle the same gray color as the cliff. A door at the bottom abruptly opened wide and when a woman stepped out, Donaldina breathed a huge sigh. He had not lied

Her elation soon turned again to apprehension. "Suppose they dinna approve of me."

"Then I shall toss them in the loch," he answered. She was serious, he noticed, so he gave her a serious answer. "I approve of you and 'tis all that matters."

"You do?"

"Aye. You are a bit annoying at times, but I have grown accustomed to it."

Any other time, she might have smiled, but she was not convinced. "I should bathe before I am presented."

He swung down off his horse, patted the horse's rump to send it on its way, and then helped her down. "Follow me," she told Arwen. The horse nodded, went to the loch to drink, and then followed.

His wife seemed hesitant to go into the water, so Wallace suggested, "Walking shall do us both good and 'twill give the lads time to tell them all about you."

"So they will not pester you with questions?"

"And you."

When he held out his hand to her, Donaldina stared at it for a time, and at last slipped her hand in his. "You have been very kind not to rush me."

"You are worth waiting for."

Somehow his words meant more to her than any she had ever heard, even from her father. "You favor me?"

"Very much."

"I see." When he began to walk, she kept her hand in his and walked beside him. "'Tis too late to run off, I suppose."

"If you find you are unhappy here, you are free to go whenever you like."

"But not alone?"

"Nay, I would send the lads with you."

She stopped and stared at him. "Why did you not say that before?"

"You dinna ask."

Donaldina rolled her eyes and started them walking again.

"You had plenty of chances, why did you stay with me?"

She quickly glanced his direction and then looked away. "I am not certain why I dinna in the beginning, and after that 'twas because we were too far away."

"Do you…" he started, but when she stopped to watch the brothers, he stopped too. As soon as they were out of the water, three women waited to greet their husbands.

"Steinn's wife is happy to see him," she said.

"Aye, and I am glad of it."

"As am I. He takes a bit of getting used to, but Steinn is a good lad. They all are." She continued to watch as the clan gathered around the brothers and it was easy to tell they wanted to know all about her. "Them," she muttered.

"What about them?"

"'Tis because of them I dinna run off in the beginning."

All at once, the clan roared with laughter, which perplexed both Wallace and his wife. "Perhaps we should not have let Obbi get there first."

She grinned, "I dinna think we could have stopped him."

"You are right, of course." He pointed to a couple walking around the loch to greet them. "'Tis Karr, the eldest brother and his wife, Catrina, who is also my sister."

Donaldina gasped. "Hani is right; Karr is even bigger than he."

"Aye, he is. If you have a heavy load, 'tis Karr you shall want to call on to carry it. He is also my second in command. He comes to give me his report."

She suddenly felt self-conscious and dropped his hand. The couple coming toward them was smiling, but she was far from confident when it came to meeting new people without her father nearby. If they had come to barter, she would know precisely how to act, but these people wanted nothing from her. Donaldina hardened her resolve and got ready.

"At last, my brother has had the good sense to marry. And are you not the most handsome lass I have yet to see. No wonder he fancies you," said Catrina, as she opened her arms and hugged Donaldina.

"Thank you," Donaldina said.

"Come, the clan waits to welcome you." Catrina fell in beside Donaldina, leaving Karr and Wallace to walk behind them.

"I need a bath," Donaldina admitted.

"As do we all. 'Tis harvest and we have worked the whole day through." Catrina leaned a little closer. "We bath in darkness where the lads cannae see us."

"I am relieved to hear that."

As they drew closer to the castle, Donaldina saw tables with drying fruit laid out and young boys standing nearby with large fans to keep the flies away. Baskets held vegetables that were being prepared to go into the cellars for winter, and two deer carcasses hung from trees waiting until the meat could be cut into strips and then dried.

Women wore scarves over their hair, long skirts, shirts with sleeves rolled up, and aprons with pockets for knives. On each of their belts hung rags on which to wipe their hands.

"You timed your return well," Karr pestered Wallace. "The harvest is nearly in."

"I am happy to hear that. We are bone tired," Wallace admitted. Not more than a moment later, several children raced up the road to throw their arms around their laird, and to get a better look at their new mistress.

Instead of running to Wallace, the youngest girl stood in the road in front of Donaldina with her hands on her hips and a scowl on her face. "I am to marry Wallace when I am grown. My mother said so."

Donaldina knelt on one knee. "I see. Yet by then he would be an elder."

The child wrinkled her forehead. "Oh, I dinna think of that." She instantly threw her arms around her new mistress. "You may have him then."

Donaldina returned the child's hug and then stood the child back a little. "Thank you. I wonder – will you be my friend?" she asked, tucking a loose strand of hair behind the child's ear. "I am in desperate need of new friends." She smiled when the child nodded and then hugged her a second time. When she stood back up, the little girl slipped her hand in Donaldina's. Happiness was, she decided the feeling of a child's hand in hers. She was not ready to admit it, but already she was happier here than she had ever been at home. She looked back to make sure her horse was following and when she did, both Wallace and Karr looked back as well.

"She named her horse Arwen," Wallace said. "Wait until you see how the mare comes to her. Wait until you hear about Ceit."

"Dinna remind me," Donaldina said. "Besides, I suspect Obbi is already telling it."

"Have we any new members?" Wallace asked.

"Three, and we lost no mothers," Karr answered.

"Good." Wallace muttered. "Perhaps someday lasses will not die giving us sons."

"Or daughters," Catrina corrected as she winked at Donaldina.

*

Inside, the castle was even more livable than Donaldina expected it to be. What she expected, exactly, she did not know, especially since she never believed there was a castle. It was very clean and since the slits were neither low nor large, there was no need of curtains, save in winter to keep out the cold. There would be no servants and she had a lot to learn before she could call herself a proper wife, but learning here suited her. Before she had a chance to see what was upstairs, her new sister-in-law came for her.

"Are you not hungry?" Catrina asked. "We have prepared a feast and your husband is already eating."

Donaldina grinned. "I could eat a bear."

There were so many new faces to see and very little point in trying to remember the names. With no wives, the three youngest brothers delighted in telling tales of their journey, and even Donaldina laughed. She sat next to Wallace and caught him looking at her from time to time, but she was used to that. At last, it was time for the women to bath. She hurried back inside the castle, gathered clothes that were cleaner than the ones she had on, and rushed out to join the other women.

*

When the baths were finished and the others had gone to their homes, Wallace stood in the doorway of the castle and watched his wife.

Candles sufficiently illuminated the main room on the bottom floor of the castle, where Donaldina stood near the lit hearth trying to dry her long, blonde hair with a woolen cloth that was newer than most.

"Feel better," he asked.

"Vastly, better," she answered. She watched him come inside, and close the door, but he did not come to her and she was relieved. She could think of a thousand little things to talk about, but none of them were of any consequence, so she decided to get what she truly wanted to know out of the way. "How is it to be?"

"How is what to be?" he asked as he walked across the room.

"Well, a lad who is tricked into marriage cannae be pleased. I assume a lad has feelings the same as a lass, and…"

Wallace let her rattle on as he went to a small table and poured each of them a goblet of ale. "He dinna trick me, he told me how to trick you."

"What?" her mouth dropped and she abruptly stopped drying her hair.

"I asked for you."

She wrinkled her brow. "Truly? But all this time, you let me believe you had been tricked. Why did you not tell me?"

"You were not ready to hear it, and therefore would not have believed me."

"She thought about that for a moment. "I suppose I would not have."

"When I asked for you, your father said you would deny me, so we set out to trick you." Wallace took the rag out of her hand and replaced it with the goblet. "I suggest you drink that."

He did not need to tell her twice. She brought the goblet to her mouth and drank half down.

"He said," Wallace continued as he laid the cloth over the back of a chair, "that if I pretended not to want you, you would yield… and your father was right." Wallace came back, clicked his goblet against hers, and then drank.

She watched him for a long moment, decided she needed more ale and drank the rest. "I thought…I mean, I…"

"I know," he said. He took the goblet from her, set both of them on the table and then touched the softness of her hair. "You were in the courtyard when we came to your village. You sat on the steps of your father's castle with the wind in your hair and a sparkle in your eyes. I had never seen a more handsome lass." He cupped his hand around the back of her neck and softly urged her to come into his arms. "You, of course, had not the least interest in me. Perhaps I found that most fetching of all."

She wanted to resist and left her hands at her side, but when he pull her close she felt that exciting feeling again. Soon, the side of her face lay against his chest. "And then?"

He took a forgotten breath and stroked the back of her hair. "And then, I watched as you encouraged your father to give us a better price."

"You knew he asked too much?"

"He asked more than we could afford."

She suddenly pulled back and frowned. "Wait, did he not bribe you with saffron?"

"Do you not hear me? I dinna need to be bribed – I wanted you." She was reluctant at first, but he finally managed to draw her close again. When he did, he kissed her on the forehead and then laid his head against the top of her. "I loved you from the first. I loved how you resisted me, how you helped the ladybug move from one leaf to another, how you cared for the wolf and..." he paused when he finally felt her arms go around him. "I even loved you when you told Conall you would have gladly married him, although I confess to being somewhat jealous."

Donaldina softly giggled.

It seemed right to be in his arms and she did like him better than she had in the beginning. He did not lie about the castle, he had been kind and undemanding, and...and it was more than right to be in his arms – it felt glorious. Never had she been so content...no content was not the right word...loved. She felt a tingle when he kissed her cheek, and when he moved his lips to her neck, she knew she would be completely his forever.

CHAPTER 8

How easy it was to become a MacGreagor. Cooking, on the other hand, was a major undertaking. Thankfully, Nikolas was more than happy to teach Donaldina. Wallace worked outside most of the day, but he managed to steal a few golden moments to come inside, kiss her and tell her he missed her. It wasn't long before she admitted she felt the same.

The other MacGreagors were friendly, she learned to wash clothes and spread them out on the tree limbs. She took time to play with the children, the cats and the dogs. She did not especially enjoy the rooster, but Obbi managed to keep it from plaguing her too much when she was outside. Sometimes she watched the edge of forest for the wolf, but apparently it had found a clan of its own.

Yet, even with all that was happiness around her, there was something missing. She just couldn't figure out what.

That night, just as she was about to climb the stairs with her husband, she suddenly grabbed her forearm and cried out in pain.

Alarmed, Wallace sat her down on the stairs, pried her hand away from her arm, and lowered the candle so he could see. There was not a mark on her. "What is it?"

"I…I dinna know. It felt like it was burning."

He thought he knew what it meant, but he said nothing.

*

Juliana did not dare cry out.

It was dark in the forest, it was not safe, and neither she nor her guards ever spoke loudly. Thankfully, her sleeves were rolled up when she reached for a bowl, and let her arm get too close to the flames. Instead of crying out, she held it with her other hand and let a tear fall from her eye. "How careless of me," she whispered and then bit her lip.

Conall quickly opened his flask and poured water on her arm. When he looked, the skin was red, but it had not been badly burned. He went to his pouch, found a small bottle of potion made from the bark of a Black Alder tree, and gently spread it on her arm. "'Tis only scorched."

Relieved, Juliana thanked him and rolled her sleeve back down.

*

The path behind the village that suffered a Viking raid, did indeed take them to the main road. In each village they came to, Conall asked if they knew how to find the MacGreagors. The first three did not, but they recalled seeing seven lads and a lass pass through their land.

The fourth clan had heard of the MacGreagors, and merely pointed up the road. In the fifth village, they were greeted by a farmer on land belonging to Clan Limond. "Aye, we know them. They live in the next village. Follow the road, cross the bridge over the river, and in a little piece, you shall come to a loch. Go around the loch, and there you shall find the MacGreagor Village."

Conall nodded his appreciation.

Juliana was so excited, the men had a hard time keeping up with her. Yet when she came to the edge of the loch, she halted her horse and gazed across the water. All her life she had longed to see the sister she lost, and now that she was this close, all sorts of things ran through her mind. She was not, however, prepared for what was to come.

*

It was three days before a group of six – five men and one woman, came up the road from the Limond village. It made the MacGreagors stop what they were doing to watch. Just in case, some of the men reached for their weapons.

Helping bathe the male children, Obbi stood with water up to his knees and also paused to watch. He waited and waited, until finally the strangers got close enough to recognize. "MacTavish!" He shouted.

"MacTavish?" Donaldina muttered. She set the knife she was using to cut vegetables on the table, wiped her hands, and then opened the door to the castle. Soon after she stepped out, Wallace came to stand beside her, and then nodded for the men to put away their weapons.

"I hope 'tis not bad news," she whispered.

Wallace kept his eyes on the woman, and as she drew closer, he had no doubt who she was. "I believe 'tis good news, my love." He put his arm around her and prayed he was right.

With her next breath, Donaldina shouted, "Conall!" She grinned when he lifted his hand to wave.

By the time the MacTavish reached the MacGreagor courtyard, all seven Viking brothers stood waiting to greet them, together with most of the rest of the clan. Conall nodded to each brother, save the tallest one whom he had never seen, and then dismounted. Before he could hand the reins to his horse to a waiting boy, Donaldina was tapping him on the shoulder.

"I am so happy to see you," said Conall. "We've a devil of a time finding you." He watched as Wallace helped Juliana down, and the rest of the MacTavish dismounted.

"Is it Father?" Donaldina worriedly asked.

"Nay, 'tis a surprise." He started to hug her and then thought better of it.

"I love surprises, but to come so far..." she finally turned to look at the woman Conall had brought with him.

Conall took Donaldina's hand and took her to the woman. "Prepare yourself for a shock, Donaldina."

"I doubt you could..."

"This is Juliana," he interrupted, "your sister."

She snickered. "Just what I need, another stepsister."

Conall shook his head. "Nay, she is your true sister. You are twins."

"What?" Donaldina asked. She looked from him, to the woman and then to her husband.

"'Tis true," Juliana said. "We were born to Elaine and Donald Bisset."

Donaldina took a step back. "Impossible, my mother died when I was four. Had I a twin, I would have known about it."

"Aye, she did die, but not when you think." Juliana took a deep breath. "We are explaining this badly, I am afraid, but there is no other way to say it. Our mother died in England shortly after we were born. Father sent she and I away, and…"

"Stop! I shall hear no more of this." Donaldina abruptly turned to go back inside and found herself in her husband's arms.

"'Tis true," he whispered.

"You knew and you dinna say?"

"We dinna know, we only suspected." Wallace motioned for everyone to go about their business. "Perhaps we best go inside." He nodded for Conall and Juliana to follow, and took his wife into the castle.

Once inside, Donaldina walked around to the other side of the table and folded her arms in a huff. "I dinna believe you. Father would not have lied to me about such a thing."

It was not the sort of greeting Juliana had hoped for. When Wallace offered her a seat on the other side of the table, she gladly sat down. "I know 'tis a shock, but I tell you true. He did." She pulled her braid around to show her sister. "My hair is dark, nor did we look alike at birth. Father accused Mother of adultery and banished us both."

Conall accepted the cup of ale Wallace handed him, and sat beside Juliana. "Donaldina, I do not always say what I know, but never have I lied to you. There have been rumors about a set of twins for years. I dinna make it up for Ceit's sake, not all of it anyway."

Donaldina didn't know what to believe. She walked to one of the window slits and stared out for a time before she turned back. "I…"

"Perhaps this will help," said Juliana. She removed a small pouch hanging from her belt, opened it, and poured a Roman coin out on the table. "Do you have one? Mother told grandfather she left one for you."

Donaldina came away from the window and stared at the coin for a very long moment, before she slowly leaned down, untied the strap around her leg, and put her coin on the table. Even that did not completely convince her. "It proves nothing…not truly."

Conall said, "Tell me, did you hear a lass shout your name in the forest?"

"Aye, we did," said Wallace. He set more goblets and a pitcher on the table, and then sat down opposite Conall.

"'Twas Mairi."

"Mairi?" Donaldina thoughtfully asked. "Aye, it was Mairi, I know that now."

"'Twas your father who cut her face," said Conall.

Donaldina gasped, and slid into the chair next to her husband. "What?"

"For telling you that your mother was not truly dead," Conall answered. "She sought to tell you the truth after you married, but she could not find you." Conall bowed his head. "Someone shot her in the back and she passed, but not before she told me what she knew."

Donaldina caught her breath. "She is dead?" Tears began to well up in her eyes. "Mairi was my only friend when I was young."

"'Tis too much for her," said Wallace. "Perhaps we should let her rest."

"Aye," Conall agreed. He stood up, opened the door for Juliana, and then followed her out.

*

Before Juliana got very far, Obbi came to meet her. "Donaldina said she only had unsightly sisters. I am happy to see she was mistaken. Are you hungry? We have plenty of fresh vegetables and ripe fruit, or perhaps you prefer ale? If we are very fortunate, my brother Nikolas shall cook a feast fit for a king."

"What I would like," she answered, "is a bath and a good night's sleep in a bed."

"We have those," Nikolas assured her. He took her arm and guided her toward the loch. "'Tis warm water this time of year. We normally bath at night with the men and women separated, but…" He followed her eyes and noticed she was looking at his brother. "He is Almoor. Pay him no mind…I hope."

"Nikolas," said Obbi, "you overwhelm her. How is she to bathe with all of us watching?"

"I am willing to turn my back," Nikolas offered with a wide grin, "but I fear we shall have to bribe my brothers."

"How many brothers do you have?" Juliana asked.

"Six. All save two are harmless."

"Harmless, is it?" she asked. "I have yet to meet a lad who is harmless. Which two?" She giggled when Nikolas pointed at Obbi and Obbi pointed at Nikolas.

*

Donaldina watched her sister through the small window, felt her husband's arms go around her from behind, and in response, lay her head back against his chest. "It cannae be true, can it?"

"Why would she come all this way just to lie," he asked.

"Then I am forced to believe Father lied to me all these years. I knew something was amiss, but why? Why did he not just tell me?"

"He feared you would not love him, I suspect. Did you not say he was unhappy with all of his wives? If he was all you had, then perhaps he felt you were all he had."

She moved out of his arms and went back to sit at the table. The vegetables waited to be cut, but she did not care. "I feel so…so abandoned and confused. Tell me it shall pass quickly."

"I know not how quickly it shall pass, but there is a lass outside who quite possibly has waited all her life to find you. Perhaps you might ask her to stay with us for a year and promise to take her back when next we barter for spices."

Donaldina felt a sudden flush of exhaustion and closed her eyes for a moment. "I have always felt something was missing. Can it be that I missed her and dinna know it?"

"'Tis more than possible."

"I have always wanted a true sister. Does she look at all like me?"

"She looks very much like you."

"She is handsome, is she not?"

"Not as handsome as you, but…"

Donaldina giggled, stood up, and went into his arms. "You are a very wise husband. Just now, I think I best rescue her from Obbi and Nikolas." She kissed his lips and hurried out the door.

Wallace walked to the door, smiled, folded his arms, and leaned against the edge of the doorway. He could not hear them, but he could see the sisters exchange a few words and then watched his wife hug

her long lost sister. When he glanced back, both Roman coins were
still on the table.

*

When it was time for the MacTavish to go home, Juliana agreed
to stay.

For nearly a week, the sisters spent every waking moment
together, learning and growing to love one another. Each was
astonished at how much alike they were, and Donaldina was saddened
that she might never know her grandfather. Perhaps he might live
another year yet, and she could see him next year. Both of them
missed not knowing their mother, but at least Juliana could tell
Donaldina what she was like.

By the third time Juliana mentioned how handsome Almoor was,
Donaldina was certain they would never be parted again.

*

Laird Donald Bisset sat with an empty pitcher turned upside down
on his table and half a goblet of ale in his hand. His hair was untidy,
his beard uncombed and what little light the smoldering hearth gave
off made his eyes a deep shade of blue. There was not enough ale in
the world to cure his affliction, for his loneliness was unbearable.

He regretted not, having banished his fifth wife nor had he a desire set her aside – for the sake of other men who might fall victim to her wickedness. What tugged at his heart now, was having listened to her when she demanded he marry Donaldina off. Bisset missed his daughter grievously, and knew finally, that she was the only one in the world who would ever truly love him. Even in his drunkenness, he understood that her sister had probably found Donaldina and told her the truth.

Now – not even Donaldina loved him.

Just one impetuous, foolish choice had ruined his entire life. Just one!

Laird Bisset's forearm felt exceedingly heavy as he lifted the goblet to his lips and tasted the last drop of ale. Suddenly, a sharp pain filled the whole of his chest, he gasped for air, his head involuntarily fell forward, and then – his eyes slowly turned from blue to the color of death.

~the end~

MORE MARTI TALBOTT BOOKS

Read Marti's historical novels in chronological order:

The Viking Series:

The Viking

The Viking's Daughter

The Viking's Son

(There is a gap of about 500 years and then the MacGreagor Clan stories continue.)

Marti Talbott's Highlander Series:

The Highlander Omnibus (Books 1-3)

Marti Talbott's Highlander Series 1

Marti Talbott's Highlander Series 2

Marti Talbott's Highlander Series 3

Marti Talbott's Highlander Series 4

Marti Talbott's Highlander Series 5

Betrothed, Book 6

The Golden Sword, Book 7

Abducted, Book 8

A Time of Madness, Book 9

Triplets, Book 10

Secrets, Book 11

Choices, Book 12

Ill-Fated Love Book 13

The Other Side of the River, Book 14

(Again, there is a 500 year gap before the MacGreagor stories continue.)

Marblestone Mansion, (Scandalous Duchess Series)

The Marblestone Mansion Omnibus (Books 1-3)

Marblestone Mansion, (Scandalous Duchess Series) Book 1

Marblestone Mansion, (Scandalous Duchess Series) Book 2

Marblestone Mansion, (Scandalous Duchess Series) Book 3

Marblestone Mansion, (Scandalous Duchess Series) Book 4

Marblestone Mansion, (Scandalous Duchess Series) Book 5

Marblestone Mansion, (Scandalous Duchess Series) Book 6

Marblestone Mansion, (Scandalous Duchess Series) Book 7

Marblestone Mansion, (Scandalous Duchess Series) Book 8

Marblestone Mansion, (Scandalous Duchess Series) Book 9

Marblestone Mansion, (Scandalous Duchess Series) Book 10

Lost MacGreagor Stories, will fill in the gap between the Highlanders and Marblestone.

Beloved Ruins

Beloved Lies

Other Marti Talbott books.

The Jackie Harlan Mysteries

Seattle Quake 9.2, Book 1

Missing Heiress Book 2

Greed and a Mistress, Book 3

The Carson Series

The Promise, Book 1

Broken Pledge, Book 2

Leanna   A short story

Keep informed about new book releases and talk to Marti on Facebook at:

https://www.facebook.com/marti.talbott

Sign up to be notified when new books are published at:

http://www.martitalbott.com

are published at:

http://www.martitalbott.com

Made in the USA
Lexington, KY
03 April 2016